Dr. Hackenbush Gains Perspective

Ginger Mayerson

The Wapshott Press

Dr. Hackenbush Gains Perspective

AIDS and Class Warfare

Dr. Hackenbush Gains Perspective

Published by
The Wapshott Press
PO Box 31513
Los Angeles, CA 90031

The Wapshott Press
www.WapshottPress.com

ISBN: 978-0-9825813-4-6

06 05 04 03 4 3 2 1

Wapshott Press logo by Molly Kiely

Cover design by Robin Austin

Also by Ginger Mayerson

Dr. Hackenbush Gets a Job

Electricland

The Pajama Boy

1984

It wasn't obvious at first, but Mabel Hackenbush, better known as Dr. Hackenbush, was a well trained and serious musician. She looked younger than her twenty-eight years, and a big pair of black horn-rim glasses took the edge off her steely gaze. Singing with *Dr. Hackenbush and her Orchestra*, she appeared to be just another chick singer, albeit one with a better than average voice and phrasing. However, there was more to her than that; not only could she read music, including symphony and opera scores, she could sight-sing, arrange for anything up to a big band, conduct, and even orchestrate. She was one of the finest products of the Grove School of Music, which in its bare-bones, stripped-down, no-frills way produced some of the best composers and arrangers in the industry. She'd done well at Grove in spite of the three strikes against her: she was a vocalist, she didn't play the piano very well, and she was female. There were no women getting screen credits in film composing in 1984, and only a few in arranging (which was a dying art—Quincy Jones and the marvelous arrangements on the "Thriller" album notwithstanding). There were few female conductors, so Hackenbush was a woman in what was still essentially a man's world. And she couldn't have cared less; her goal had been to get the best musical education she could afford as quickly as possible and the mind-numbingly, life-crushing Composition and Arranging Program at Grove only took a year to complete. Thank God for that; after a year of poverty, sleep deprivation and driving to the valley almost every day, she was ready for a new life. After Grove, she managed the music industry by ignoring it. She and her baritone ukulele made themselves welcome in every jazz standards-loving club and lounge in the city. When she hooked up with the dancer Shorty Smith, they became the must-have act at every chic venue and upscale party in the county. Sidemen came and went, but the core act was Dr. Hackenbush and Smith.

Or had been. About a year ago, Eddy Lee, guitar player and frontman of the Eddy Lee Trio asked them to join him, Cody Cole on bass and a cat named Ross on drums, and make it a quartet or quintet, depending on one's point of view. They'd met one night when Hackenbush was singing serious jazz (she could do that, too) and Eddy was sitting in. It was as close to love at first sight as Hackenbush ever got. Eddy was in love, too; when she joined the band, he changed the name to *Dr. Hackenbush and her Orchestra*. Hackenbush figured if that wasn't love, she didn't know what was. The drummer and bass player eventually accepted her and Shorty, mainly because Hackenbush and Shorty got them a lot more gigs than they'd been getting as a pure jazz trio. Yeah, the Hackenbush and Shorty shtick was a little goofy, but man, could she sing and, man, could they dance.

Which is what they were doing that very Sunday afternoon at the Los Angeles Photography Center. Shorty was in the money enough to afford ten bucks an hour for three hours on a good floor and plenty of room to trip the light fantastic in. A meticulous choreographer, he didn't let Mabel get away with being lazy in rehearsals. She was a hesitant dancer until she learned her steps and then she was fine; prone to improvise, but Shorty almost had her out of that bad habit.

"Mabel, there's still only four beats in that bar," he said over the metronome.

"I know, Shorty, I know," she rasped at him. "How about a break? I can't feel my feet anymore."

He agreed and she promptly stepped outside for a cigarette. "You might last longer, dear, if you didn't smoke," he observed.

"I'd kill people if I didn't smoke," she observed back at him.

Since there was no comeback to this, Shorty left her to smoke in peace. He went back inside to look at the exhibit of photos of some landscape he didn't recognize. Art was the last thing he thought about at the Photography Center; Hackenbush was the first. They'd met there, two years ago: Shorty was dancing two solos in a little revue set to Cole Porter songs and Hackenbush and her baritone ukulele were the majority of the music. The show was produced, directed and choreographed by Gregg Schroedingmeier, now long-gone from the LA dance scene, whose main complaint was that Hackenbush's voice got more attention than his dancing, his lighting, and everything he could take credit for. Shorty was surprised the egomaniac didn't take credit for the voice God gave the woman, but Hackenbush's voice was a thing unto itself. Soft, but powerful in its softness and vulnerable in its strength. Shorty eventually figured out the ukulele, which she could play credibly, was more prop than instrument, even if it went perfectly with her smoky, sultry voice.

After the performance, he'd tracked her down and asked her to dance with him. At first she said no, she didn't dance, don't ask her. But he kept asking and eventually, when a paying gig came along, she agreed, and found that not only could she dance, she loved it.

Shorty was a patient soul and Hackenbush loved him dearly for it. He made her look like a better dancer than she was and made her into a better dancer than she thought she could ever be. So as not to provoke him and because she really was interested in this complicated new dance he'd concocted, she only smoked half her Pall Mall. "Okay, boss, I'm back on the clock," she said, picking a shred of tobacco off her tongue.

Shorty giggled and turned the metronome back on. He worked them hard for another hour and then they had dinner at a Thai place across from the Samsara School of Oriental Medicine on Third near Rampart.

"You think I ought to let those Chinese doctors stick pins in me, Shorty?" Hackenbush asked over a plate of panang curry. "My right shoulder and thumb are killing me."

"I think you type too much, Mabel, and should carry your purse on your left side," Shorty said.

"Yeah, maybe," she said. "I'll be typing less when we start the new gig next weekend."

Shorty's mouth was full, so he just nodded. Eddy and Mabel had landed the band a peach of a long-term, high-paying gig in Santa Monica. A good room for music and dancing and it was a chain of hotels, so they might be in the money for quite a while. "We can all save a little money on this gig," he said when he could.

"I'll be saving a little money when I move in with Eddy," she said. "You know what they say about how two can live as cheaply as one. I'm giving my fucking landlord notice next week."

"Hey, congratulations! I would dance at your wedding, Mabel."

"You dance at everything, Shorty, my wedding would not be exceptional. Except that it would be my wedding," she murmured. She was distracted with toting up the check, adding 23%, and dividing it in half. "And don't jump the gun so fast, darlin', we're just moving in together."

"Well, it's nice," Shorty said, digging in his wallet for money. "You really love this guy, don't you?"

"'Deed I do, Shorty, 'deed I do."

They smiled across the table at each other. Shorty had seen her through some ugly, tawdry affairs, one or two married men (until she finally learned that there really is no trouble like another woman's man), and months of snarling celibacy and borderline man-hating. He occasionally wondered why she didn't just switch to women, but the lesbians that made the rare pass at her were politely, but firmly, rebuffed. Shorty figured Eddy Lee got in under her radar because they had a foundation of mutual musical respect to fall safely in love on.

Hackenbush was happy; dear God, at last she was happy. All the years of scuffling, starving, working day jobs, suffering, and moments of pure musical bliss, followed by long stretches of creative growth, when all the work paid off and the music was as free and easy as breathing. In all those years, she'd always felt threatened, scared, and watched her back. Shorty was the first person in LA she felt safe enough with to let her guard down and relax a little. And now Eddy: Lordy, did that man make her feel safe and loved. She carried the warmth of his arms through the hours without him. His embrace was the home she thought she'd never find, and she knew it would be there when she got back to him. His love was one of the few things outside of herself she could count on. It was always something to look forward to at the end of the day, there was Eddy Lee, home, and all the peace and love in that.

She had thought that when she found this kind of love, she'd understand all those happy songs. It was not the case. No song could capture what she felt, not even words and music could do it justice. So, she reasoned, either what she had with Eddy was unique or this kind of once-in-a-lifetime love was just bigger than thirty-two bars and a verse could express. Hackenbush now had a better understanding of the dark songs of lost and hopeless love. She felt she knew more about them from her observations of others' emotional shipwrecks and her own varied and personal experience. She still sang those songs, they were some of the greatest songs ever written; but she now sang them with more hope than tragedy, in an effort to tell her audiences that life is sad, but it might not always be. She kept the message subtle, because she didn't want to get bashed in the face by some heartbroken poor devil who hated her for her happiness. And Hackenbush could dig it: when she was really down, the last thing she wanted was to hear about somebody else's joy. It was petty of her, but there it was.

"What's Ross gonna do?" Shorty asked.

Ross shared a house with Eddy and Hackenbush hadn't really thought about what he'd do when she moved in. "I dunno, d'you think he'd want my place?"

"Echo Park is a lot different than Mid Wilshire."

"Well, he's a big guy, he'll work it out," she said gathering up her things. "Are you coming to see me in my servitude tomorrow night?"

"No, but I'll get there one night," Shorty said, holding the door for her. "One doesn't hear you sing art songs very often."

"Yeah, I know."

"You should know better than to bet on Lola Rae," he said.

"I was betting on love, Shorty, Lola just happened to be involved," she said, sourly. "Although I should know better than to have anything to do with that crazy woman. Six months ago she nearly broke my neck."

"How?" Shorty asked. He was a big fan of the willowy, blond dancer, but knew she had certain eccentricities and gave them a wide berth. One of them was that she mauled

Hackenbush every chance she got.

"She grabbed my hair at Bart's Bar and Grill to tell me she liked the way I sang 'Moonglow'," Hackenbush said, opening her VW Bug's door for him. "She could have just told me, but no, she had to bend me nearly backwards to tell me."

"Well, we are talking about Lola Rae, aren't we?"

"Yes. Thank God Cody held me up while she did it." Hackenbush shuddered at the memory. "I might have been snapped like a twig."

Shorty didn't comment on Hackenbush's un-twig-like figure; few twigs of his acquaintance had quite so many curves as she did. He merely smiled, and said he figured Lola was in the Bay Area for good. "She's knocking them dead up there."

"Dancing?"

"Of course!"

She dropped him at his new place in Hollywood. It was a nice apartment in a deco building on Bronson. She wondered how he could afford it and she suspected he was being kept, but was too arrogant to ask him. Besides, if he wanted her to know what he was up to, he'd tell her; until then she'd pretend not to give a damn.

Shorty had mixed luck with the men in his life; they were either givers or takers. Hackenbush thought Shorty was a great guy and could never quite figure out why he couldn't find a man that was a bit more balanced and settle down. "Count your blessings, Hackenbush," she reminded herself as she merged onto the 101 Freeway south. "Not everyone is as lucky as you and Eddy."

That night the band played a wedding reception in Marina del Rey. Hackenbush tried to put the idea that she might have one of these one day out of her head.

"You looked nice tonight, Mabel," Cody told her when they were packing up.

Hackenbush had on her basic-black-combat-casual-job evening gown; legions of waiters had spilled drinks and food on it and it all came out in a cold water wash on delicate. "Thanks, Cody, I do try to look nice at these jobs," she said. "How'd I sound?"

"You sounded nice, too."

"Just nice?"

"It's just a casual, Mabel, save it for the gigs," Cody said, zipping his bass cover up. "I hear you lost that bet."

"News travels fast," she said. "That's what I get for betting on Lola Rae to do anything sane."

"I hear she's comin' back," Cody said.

"Figures. You gonna come see me in my suffering?" she asked.

"I might fall by. Arty said he's tired of being the only Negro at his nightclub."

Hackenbush shrugged, but Ross thought it was funny.

"He said that? Hell, Cody, maybe I should come by, too, except lute music gives me hives," he managed to say between guffaws.

"Laugh it up, cats, at least dinner comes with the gig and you know how good the food is there," she said on her way out. Eddy was packed up and tapping his foot waiting for her to get with it. They went back to her place; she'd spent part of her afternoon cleaning it up and changing the sheets.

Hackenbush was going to be on a tight schedule that week. Her temp job in Glendale ended at five; she had to get home to Echo Park, warm up, change into the modest and severe black silk jersey gown she'd picked up secondhand, which she now thought of as her "recital" dress. Then she had to be in Pasadena at seven to sing art songs with the lute-playing rocket scientist from the Jet Propulsion Laboratory.

The bet she'd lost was that Lola Rae and Mark Wilson would stay together even if Lola went to dance in San Francisco for a month. Hackenbush had bet on love and lost because Mark took a gig in Japan and left town a few weeks later; Lola still wasn't back. Hackenbush could be forgiven: she was in love herself and her judgment was a little off. But off in a good way, it was "La Vie en Rose", something she'd never believed in, much less thought would ever happen to her.

But back in the present and due to losing this bet, she had this stupid gig at Inn Arty's wine bar in Pasadena with Dr. Herbert Friederman, physicist, Ph.D., and lute player. He'd

been admiring her at a party and guitar player Al Juarez had
made a week of Hackenbush singing art songs with him the
payoff if she lost. The payoff if she won was that Al would be
standing up there singing in badly-accented French. Now, that
would have been something to see. The deal had been that if
Lola came or didn't come back by the end of May, she and Al
would pressure Arty into giving Dr. Friederman a week of
weeknights. Dr. Friederman mailed them photocopies of the
songs that he immediately set to perfecting on his lute.
Difficult to know how much science was lost due to this
wacky errand. Hackenbush was annoyed to have to learn the
very songs she'd so successfully avoided all her vocalist life.
But a deal's a deal, and she was a woman of her word so there
she was. Professional to her sensible shoes, she'd even forked
over some real cash to a vocal coach, just to see if she was
doing it right. She was, and lessons were fun, if expensive
and all the way down in Newport Beach. Anyway, after the
first gig, Eddy would be waiting at her place and this would
give her courage to get though the two and a half hours, with
breaks and dinner, of Ravel, Debussy, Fauré, and other dead
French guys she'd never heard of before, and never wanted to
hear of again. At least Hackenbush was singing well, in
badly-accented French, but well, nevertheless. She gave her
ukulele those nights off; a lute and uke sounded too much like
some kind of Hawaiian hippie folk concert to her and she
needed to concentrate on her singing too much to play
competently. Mostly she just wanted to get through the night
with as little hassle as possible.

Monday night was quiet. Arty's was filled with
gourmets who just wanted a quiet evening of good food.
Hackenbush and Friederman got a few dirty looks as they set
up, but then became wallpaper, which had always been the
plan. It was an okay gig; almost a dress rehearsal due to Dr.
Friederman's nerves and fine tuning in a few places.
Hackenbush had to hand it to him, though; he was a serious
musician, even if she didn't care for lute music. Much to her
surprise, because she was focused on singing and not the
audience (it wasn't that kind of crowd anyway), they got a
smattering of applause after each song. It was probably
people who just had their hands free between courses, or it

might have been some real appreciation. Hackenbush didn't have a problem with the music; it was beautiful music, but just not something she could really connect with. She was a singer, so she sang as well as she could, which was very well indeed. Arty fed her one of the best steaks of her life and she was with Eddy by ten.

The job in Glendale was data entry, something Hackenbush could do in her sleep, so it was almost a restful four days. The accounting manager, Ms. Metzger, was a weird combination of grateful and resentful toward the three temps Solutionations sent out to deal with the backlog. She was grateful they were there and doing the work, but resentful that she couldn't manage her own staff well enough to get it done in the first place. Hackenbush could see why that might be so; Metzger was trying to be friends with everyone and was getting taken advantage of right and left. The silly woman had been by Hackenbush's desk three times the first morning to make sure she was comfortable, knew what she was to do, and to see if she needed anything. All this did was interrupt Hackenbush's rhythm on the 10-key and the answers were simple: yes, thanks, this office chair is just fine; yes, thanks, I'll just input this two-foot stack of two-month-old invoices and then start on the box of filled orders on the floor; yes, thanks, I need you to leave me the fuck alone, thanks. Okay, she didn't say that. She liked the people at Solutionations too much to do that to them. She'd been working there for years and would need to again someday. No matter how well music jobs were going, there were unpredictable dry spells where a temp job just had to tide you over.

Hackenbush was on this one as a favor to Valerie MacGruder, whom she'd been working for out of Solutionations for years. Recently, Val had been promoted to branch manager, which was a mixed blessing for her temps: it meant they'd have to break in a new temp wrangler. So far, the chick who'd taken over Val's workload, Anna Kodaly, was cool. Hackenbush hadn't talked to her that much because she'd been mostly making a living as a musician.

But Val was almost a friend and when, from her exalted new job title, she personally called Hackenbush to save a big account, how could Hackenbush refuse? After all the years of being first call on the best paying jobs, she owed Val at least four days on an annoying job. It turned out that Val must have really been in trouble because Linda Lim and Sandy Garner, sculptor and pianist and two of the finest temps in greater LA, were on the job with her. This meant the lunches at the Pearl Café on Maryland Street were fun, at least.

"I hear you and Eddy Lee are shacking up," Linda said over her burger on Tuesday.

"Next month," Hackenbush said. "How'd you hear?"

"I heard from Suzy Reed, who heard it from Shorty," Linda said. "So it must be true."

"I heard it from Renee Soleil last night at the Oak Room," Sandy put in. "She was singing with Lewis Lewis."

Hackenbush shot her a wary look; Eddy and Renee had been lovers well before Hackenbush knew either of them. Renee was a pretty good singer, so being a vocalist and Eddy's ex-flame made her double trouble in Hackenbush's books. Although, she never asked Eddy about Renee, and he never brought her up, Hackenbush had learned from gossip that Renee had nearly sucked—literally and figuratively—the life out of Eddy when they were together.

"I've no idea where she heard it," Sandy added, staring down Hackenbush's scowl. "If Shorty knows, the whole dance scene knows, and you know how fast good gossip spreads."

"What did she say?" Hackenbush asked.

"Well, the first thing she said was that she wanted to hear you at Arty's because she's always suspected you can sing when you don't have to clown with Shorty and front the band."

"That fucking bi–"

"It was a compliment, Mabel," Sandy said in her no-bullshit voice. It was the voice she used on conductors who couldn't find "one" and singers who needed a kick in the ass to stay focused. "We're coming to see you tonight."

"Oh great." Hackenbush gave up on her Club sandwich and lit a cigarette. "What'd she say about Eddy?"

"She said she was impressed." Sandy waved Hackenbush's smoke away. "She never got that far with him, so you must really have it. She wondered about Eddy, she said he was a little more skittish when they were together, but people change, and he must've found the right woman to settle down with."

"She said all that?" Hackenbush asked.

"Well, she also said 'God help Hackenbush, Eddy's ninety percent bastard and one hundred percent guitar player'."

"That sounds more like her," Hackenbush said, over Linda laughing so hard she choked on her coffee. "She really is a bitch," she added, whacking the sculptor between her shoulder blades. "Ow, Linda, you got a back like a rock."

"All those years of sculpture," Linda said, between coughs.

"Anyway, Mabel, Renee and I are coming to Arty's tonight and I told her, so I'll tell you: be nice," Sandy said.

"Me? I'm not gonna fuck with the Renee and Sandy show, believe me," Hackenbush said, already thinking of subtle ways to insult Renee without pissing off Sandy. "Besides, Arty's got the best food in town, there's no way I'm messing up that relationship with a catfight in his club."

"You? In a catfight? How interesting." Linda wiped her lips and accepted the Pall Mall Hackenbush offered her.

"Well, I haven't been in one since High School and I was the big loser," Hackenbush admitted. "The PE teacher had to rescue me."

"How humiliating," Linda said, looking at her watch. "Back to the data entry mines, girls."

"So, I'll see you tonight?" Hackenbush asked Sandy in the elevator.

"As far as I know right now, you will."

"Maybe me, too," Linda put in. "This sounds interesting and I like lute music."

"You do?" Hackenbush was a little shocked to hear this from the most modern of modern sculptors. On the other hand, Dr. Friederman's lute playing was growing on her. "By the way, the singing is pretty damn good, too," she added as the elevator doors opened.

Nobody ventured to crack wise; they were all in their professional temp roles, gliding back into data entry, word processing, filing and whatever the hell else needed doing.

Ms. Metzger stayed in her office all afternoon, and this was an extra blessing as far as Mabel, Linda and Sandy were concerned.

Inn Arty's was in a large, tastefully decorated storefront on a quiet street in west Pasadena. It was filled with white wood, dark carpet, soft lights and softer music. Although the carpet made it a dead room acoustically, even Hackenbush had to admit it was a lovely space. The little stage for musicians was barely big enough for Hackenbush, Dr. Friederman and his lute. It was too close to the kitchen door for Hackenbush to be happy. But she was not there to be happy: she was there to pay off a bet, sing well, and eat excellent food. That night Arty gave them buttery grilled shrimps, garlicky mashed potatoes, quiche with ham and broccoli, and spicy stir-fried green beans. Nothing was as good as getting paid to sing, but Hackenbush felt that this was pretty damn close.

The word seemed to be out that lute music didn't cause cancer and Hackenbush was singing like an angel, so every musician with nothing better to do was at Inn Arty's that night. Everyone except Eddy Lee, who'd not only had to listen to his babe learning these songs, but had had to listen to her bitch about having to learn these songs. He'd politely offered his opinion of her version of "Beau Soir" when asked, and was ignored. That song had gotten very old for Ed after the tenth hearing anyway. However, Hackenbush did hope he'd find the will to fall by to hear her sing at least one set and have a glass of wine with her.

Renee and Sandy blew in during the last set and ordered dessert. When the dessert cart came around, Hackenbush saw Sandy take a piece of pecan pie and Renee a slice of chocolate cake. Hackenbush knew the pecan pie was good, she'd had it on Monday, but the chocolate cake looked too rich for her. Renee only managed to finish half of her slice, so it must be very rich indeed. Renee Soleil was a big woman with a big voice and huge other appetites. And so, seeing Renee's experience, Hackenbush decided she probably didn't want anything to do with that chocolate cake, now or ever.

Dr. Friederman cleared his throat; in her reverie she'd missed her cue. He improvised a four bar phrase, something

Hackenbush hadn't known could be done on a lute, and swung around to her entrance again. Dr. Friederman was turning out to be cooler than she'd thought and she found herself singing well because one should always sing well, but also to please him. She wouldn't miss this gig, but she wouldn't have any regrets when it was over.

After the gig, while Dr. Friederman was packing up, Sandy waved her over and bought her a glass of wine. Sandy looked a little nervous, causing Hackenbush to believe Renee might have been being bitchy. Renee was a bit too blasé, especially after all that chocolate, and Hackenbush was left to sip her wine and wonder if she and the singer were going to be ladies like Sandy, or if they were just going to ignore each other.

Renee cracked first. "You sound good up there, Mabel," she said, making eye contact and smiling politely.

"Ah, thank you, just shifting gears," Hackenbush said, also making eye contact, but smiling loftily as she imagined Maria Callas must have done more than once in her career.

"Were you trained?" Renee asked in an undertone, as if it was something to be ashamed of.

"As a matter of fact I did take a few lessons from a guy in Newport Beach to get ready for this gig," Mabel said, thinking this was awfully civilized for Eddy Lee's she-devil ex-girlfriend.

"What dedication. That's a longish drive, Mabel, what did Eddy do while you were gone?" the She-devil asked.

Hackenbush tried not to flaunt her happiness, but Renee had it coming. "Oh, practiced, watched TV, whatever guys do on their own. He did take the train down to Santa Ana and had dinner with me and my dad. Sort of a welcome to the family thing. My dad seems to like him as much as he likes anyone," she said, hoping her smile was smug and obnoxious.

It was both and then some. Renee's eyes got very cold on the other side of the table. "Oh? Will Eddy be converting to Judaism for you?"

"Oh, dear me, no," Hackenbush cooed, or hoped she was cooing and not snarling. "He'd have to convert to Zen Judaism and he's already that anyway."

"Tsk, oh, honestly, Hackenbush," Sandy sighed. "Bad

things happen to people who make up religions." Sandy had the advantage of being able to ignore her Catholic background.

"Tosh, Sandy, this is a well-established, completely unorganized faith," Hackenbush laughed at her.

"Oh yeah? Tell me a Zen Judaist joke," Sandy demanded.

"Well, there aren't any," Hackenbush said. "And if there were, no one would get them."

"Huh?" Sandy and Renee said in stereo.

"See?" Hackenbush folded her hands. She unfolded them to wave good-night at Dr. Friederman.

For Hackenbush, it was simple: she just wanted a God she didn't have to work too hard to believe in. An abstract God she could reliably and quietly worship, Who didn't make too many demands on her and upon Whom she returned the favor. If God would keep an earthquake from swallowing Los Angeles, Hackenbush would praise that God and take care of herself and her pals.

"I'll have to think about that one," Sandy finally said. Renee just nodded.

"Well, I have to go home," Hackenbush said, omitting that Eddy Lee was waiting for her there. She figured Renee had had enough for one night.

On their morning break, Sandy told her she sounded pretty good on those art songs. "Hard work, eh?"

"Yeah, hard to sing and not much room for my personality," Hackenbush admitted. Eddy had stood her up last night, claimed he was too tired to come over to her place, or for her to come to his. She was trying to keep the frown out of her voice. This was probably her punishment for flaunting her happiness a little to Renee, damn her.

"You and your personality were doing fairly well up there," Sandy said. "But you've got nice color in your voice I never noticed before. You and that lute player ought to get it on tape while you can."

Just to get rid of her, Hackenbush said she thought it was a good idea. But, because she understood Sandy's compliment, she added it to her 'To-Do' list, albeit way down near the bottom of the list. "Hey, Linda! Where were–?"

"I'm coming tonight! I'm coming tonight!" Linda raised her very muscular arms defensively in front of her. As if anyone would ever take her on; she could press her own weight and crack walnuts in her bare hands.

"Oh yeah? Can you bring your tape recorder?"

Ross and Cody also showed up that night. Either Wednesdays were naturally busy or the word was out the music was good. The food was always good, but some people need extra incentive. Arty sat down and had dinner with the drummer and bass player, something Hackenbush had never seen him do with any other customer. He was a gracious and considerate host, but kept his professional, restaurateur distance. However, with Ross and Cody, Arty relaxed and let himself enjoy his chef's cooking and the classier part of his own wine rack. Hackenbush smiled and waved, but kept her distance so as not to interrupt their peaceful island of Negritude or whatever it was.

She and Dr. Friederman were in the midst of their own good dinner—lobster bisque, roast beef, glazed carrots, huge baked potatoes stuffed with cheese, broccoli, pressed garlic, ham, sour cream and chives, and they skipped dessert, that's how much food it was—but she discreetly observed that Arty pulled out all the stops for Ross, Cody and himself. She wanted to ask Friederman if he thought that was duck they were eating—it was dim in Arty's and Hackenbush didn't have the best angle on the table—but he was off in some reverie, probably involving a lute solo, so she left him alone.

She sauntered up to sit with them on her first break. "Can a white girl get a seat at this table?" she asked. "How was dinner, cats?" She waved at Linda, just coming in, who was waving her tape recorder at her.

"Delicious! Especially the duck part," Cody sighed. "That man in that kitchen can sure cook some." He and Ross nodded happily at each other.

"Speaking of," Arty said, rising. "I better get on with my chores." He winked at Hackenbush and made his way around the room, tending his customers, many of whom were old friends.

"I hope the singing isn't interfering with your digestion," Hackenbush said pointedly.

"The singing," Ross said, matching her tone, "is effete, decadent, and would destroy decent society if left unchecked." He paused so Hackenbush could roll her eyes. "Puts you in a bind, Mabel, you have to sing what the composer meant, not your idea of what the composer meant, or it all falls apart. You might as well be singing in a straight jacket up there."

"Oh, come now, Ross," Hackenbush said. "I'd never get my ribcage open enough in a straightjacket, why else do you think I'm wearing this baggy schmata?" They laughed. "So, it's not the singing, it's the material you don't like?"

"Yeah," he said. "It's not a secret you can sing, Mabel, and to tell the truth, I never knew you had so much voice in there, but it's what you do with a song that makes it special and there is no room for that with this stuff." He waved dismissively, which meant end of subject.

"I liked that one song," Cody said.

"Which one?" she asked.

"The one around eight-fifteen." Cody smiled serenely, but Hackenbush couldn't tell if he was smiling at her, his own joke, or the dessert cart heading their way.

"Heard Renee was in last night," Ross asked softly. "How'd it go?"

"Oh fine," Hackenbush said as breezily as she could manage. "Watch out for the chocolate cake, even Renee couldn't finish it." She excused herself and went over to sit with Linda, and also to make sure there was a tape in the cassette player. Linda was a great sculptor, but only a so-so recording engineer.

Glancing over at Ross, she found him watching her. Cody was deep in some pecan pie, and her lightness had probably fooled him, but not Ross. If Eddy was too tired to come over last night, then he must have been at the place he shared with Ross, and that might have seemed as strange to Ross as it did to Hackenbush. Add in the fact that she, as well as Ross, knew Eddy wasn't gigging much this week, and still hadn't come to see her sing; it was bugging her and Ross could see it. This bugged her even more. "What, Linda?" she asked, realizing the artist had asked her something.

"I said, who's that gorgeous guy with Shorty?"

Hackenbush followed her nod and, lo and behold, Shorty

Smith was being seated at an intimate table for two with a gorgeous older man. Hackenbush sketched Shorty a wave and got a stagey wink back. 'Must be the new sugar daddy,' Hackenbush thought, but said, "Must be the new boyfriend. I was wondering why he wasn't around so much lately."

"Don't blame him," Linda said, trying not to stare. "Shorty sure can pick them, can't he?"

"Yeah, and they sure can pick him. It's keeping them that's the tough part." Hackenbush caught Dr. Friederman's eye and they both rose to return to the stage.

She sent a rueful smile Ross's way and sang.

Eddy was playing a solo cocktail lounge gig at Dino's in East Pasadena that night. After the show, most of the crowd migrated over there. Hackenbush, Dr. Friederman and a few woodwind players sat in. Eddy seemed glad to see everyone, but it was such a wholesale invasion of his gig, he really had no choice but to be cool about it. Hackenbush only stayed until 11:30; she had to work the next day. She didn't say anything about the previous night, just gave him a comradely slap on the back, said, "See ya," and split. Unwilling to bet on whether he'd show up later, she went home and acted like it was any other night before a workday. So of course he showed up at 1AM, but that was just fine, if not more than fine, with Hackenbush.

Thursday was the last day on the temp job. Sue Metzger had gone out on stress leave so the office manager signed her time card and thanked her. "Wish we had a few more like you around here, Mabel," she said. "If you're ever looking for perm, don't forget us," she added, handing Mabel her card. To be polite, Hackenbush said she wouldn't forget them, and then did well before she got home.

That night was also the last night of her gig at Inn Arty's. She would miss Arty's cooking and even Dr. Friederman's lute playing, but she would not miss this crazy art songs gig. On the last break, Arty very casually sounded her about doing another week.

"Nah, but Dr. Friederman could carry this gig on his own," she said.

"That's what I thought, but he said I had to ask you anyway," Arty said.

"What a gent! No, thanks though, I'm retiring from the art songs scene, but grab Dr. Friederman while you can."

Arty said he fully intended to. Hackenbush wished him good luck—she was really going to miss the food on this gig, alas—and was about to remount the stage for the last set of the last night of the gig when Eddy and Cody came in. "Hey, guys!"

Cody split off to talk quietly to Arty and Eddy headed for his babe. "Mabel, we got called for a casual at the Biltmore," he said, all business. "We have to be there in half an hour. I picked up your baritone ukulele on the way. Ross and Shorty are there setting up right now."

Reflexively, Hackenbush looked at Arty, who nodded and gave her thumbs-up. She glanced at the oblivious Dr. Friederman, and Arty headed over to explain the situation. "Oh fuck, Eddy, do I have time to go home and change out of this dumb dress?" she asked, now that she could concentrate on important stuff.

"No, but I grabbed a dress for you at your place," Eddy said, smugly, and pulled a few yards of satin from his shoulder bag.

"Ed, that's a nightgown. But nice try," she said, resigned to her modest and severe black dress. Oh well, it was just a casual anyway. She apologized to Dr. Friederman, who took it like a man; she hugged him and said she'd enjoyed working with him. In many ways she had; that gig wouldn't be a bad memory, just an interesting one. And one she'd pretty much filed away by the time they got to the Emerald Ballroom at the Biltmore downtown. It turned out to be a great casual, in spite of her dress.

Hackenbush got to sleep in that Friday morning; the band's new gig started that night and she'd wanted to rest up for it. So she breezed into Solutionations after lunch to talk to Valerie about her hiatus from temping.

She said hi to Anna Kodaly and handed her that week's timecards for herself, Linda and Sandy.

"I don't know how you people get clients to sign timecards in advance," Anna said, checking the hours.

"Sandy and Linda inspire nothing but trust, Anna,"

Hackenbush said. "And the clients know they can take it out of Solutionations' hide if the temps flake on Friday."

"Which has never happened," Anna shot back.

"And likely never will. We're devoted little Solutionistas; we need you" Mabel said, figuring the next time she'd need Solutionations, Anna would have moved on. Between flaky temps and creepy management, turnover on temp agency personnel was shocking; anybody with a brain fled in six months, usually to a job that was just as bad, but the novelty made it bearable for a while. However, temp bookers usually took their list of A-list temps with them to the next job. This was how a good temp could end up working at half a dozen agencies, following their meal ticket.

Hackenbush figured she'd follow Anna to her next move, if and when she had to work temp jobs again. But, for the foreseeable future, Hackenbush was done temping, and this was great news for her, not for Valerie MacGruder, the branch manager, and Hackenbush was there to tell her in person.

Valerie was hardly a creepy manager. She did her best to keep the profits flowing up the Solutionations corporate ladder and keep her staff and temps happy. She had a reliable bunch working for her at the moment, so she was sorry to see Hackenbush go.

"How long did you say you think you'll be unavailable?" she asked, trying to take it in.

"Well, we're booked through October, then the holidays are very busy, and then we figure after the new year there might be cruise ship work..."

"Six months?"

"More like a year, Val, this hotel chain likes us a lot, and they've got lots of places for us to gig," Hackenbush said, knowing a year was a lifetime in Valerie's business.

And Val knew this perfectly well, too. "We'll miss you, Mabel," she said, rising to shake her hand. "Anna will miss you a lot. You've almost got her trained."

Hackenbush laughed politely and left. She liked Val; she'd been working for her since Val had had Anna's job. It was nice to see her succeed: she'd been one of the few temp bookers to understand, if not exploit, the fact that not all the best temps had a corporate mentality. This had paid off well for everyone; Val got promoted and Solutionations kept scores of struggling artists in all fields more or less solvent.

She said good-bye to Anna and headed for Hollywood and Shorty. There were a few errands she wanted to run before she picked up her dance partner. She was down to her last fifth of tequila and wanted to stop by Liquortopia on Fountain Street and pick up a case. Not that Hackenbush could drink a case of tequila by herself; she had lots of friends to help her and parties to take a gift bottle to. She was also in the planning stages of a housewarming for her and Eddy after they moved in together in June. It was also cheaper to buy it by the case, and Hackenbush economized wherever she could and whenever she had the money to do so. After she got Shorty and they had a very late lunch, she'd swing by her place and pick up her gown and ukulele for the gig that night. The plan was to meet at Eddy's place in Mid-Wilshire and go in Ross' van.

"... so, um, that's it, I'm done. Bye." Eddy hung up the phone and turned to find Ross standing in the doorway.

"Oh, shit, Ed, you gotta be kidding." Ross, standing in the doorway, stared hard at the suitcase, guitar case and then back at his housemate.

"Nah." Eddy brushed his greasy bangs out of his eyes and picked up his stuff.

"What about the gig?" Ross asked, standing in his way.

Eddy shrugged. "Sorry, Ross."

"And Mabel?"

He blew out a long breath. "She's why I gotta split," and looked Ross in the eye.

"We could get another singer."

"It's more complicated than that, Ross, so excu–"

"This has been coming on for awhile, hasn't it?" Ross didn't move out of his way. "Why now?"

"I waited too long, got too involved, and now I gotta go."

Ross argued with him a little longer, but eventually realized Eddy was not going to see sense, let alone do the right thing, and he stepped out of his way. He waited until the car started up, pulled out of the driveway, and then waited some more. He wasn't waiting for anything, he was just letting some time go by before he had to call Hackenbush and break the news to her.

The phone was ringing when Mabel and Shorty got back to her place. "Get that Shorty, okay?" She had an arm full of tequila and the leftovers from lunch. Although she kept trying, she could never eat much before a gig.

"Oh, hi Ross," Shorty said and then he was listening very closely.

Since Shorty wasn't holding the phone out to her, Mabel pushed the play button on her machine.

"'Hi, Mabel, look...'" Hackenbush landed hard on her knees before the end of the message. The message looped in her head, repeating more slowly than what was on the tape, and every repetition coiled something inside her chest tighter and tighter until she was having trouble getting a full breath. Her body went limp and she slumped against the phone stand. A blurry darkness began to close in on her; she was barely able to focus on the bottle of tequila she was reaching for. All she knew was that she had to get the bottle open before she started to shake, and get as much tequila down before the darkness overwhelmed her. She just wanted to blunt the hard and final edges Eddy's message. It wasn't the words tearing her up, they were Eddy's usual bland words, but the vibe: it was over for him, done for him, he was walking away, and she was alone, on her own again, would never feel his touch, never hear his voice again except for this message, and that was more than she could handle sober just then.

"M– Mabel? It's Ross," Shorty said when the message finished. He held out the phone to her. He, too, was reeling from Eddy's message.

"Tell him to fuck off." She was too busy drinking tequila straight out of the bottle to talk to anyone just then.

Shorty in person and Ross and Cody in phone calls tried to get her to see reason, or at least save the binge for after the gig. Eventually the screaming and crying got on their nerves and they gave up. Shorty stuck around until she passed out, just to make sure she didn't hurt herself. Ross called Al

Juarez and Renee Soleil to fill in for Eddy and Hackenbush. There was no way anyone could fill in for Shorty. Unfortunately, these game, but last-minute replacements gave the very elegant hotel gig a jam session vibe and *Dr. Hackenbush and her Orchestra*, Hackenbush, Smith and Lee in abstentia, were fired half way through the evening.

"God damn Eddy Lee," was all Ross had to say about it, and then he was too busy scrambling for work to do much else. Over the next few weeks he occasionally looked in on Mabel to see if she'd sobered up enough to work again. He was impressed and somewhat alarmed that she could drink so much and not be dead yet. The booze was taking its toll; she looked like shit, but he figured she felt even worse. It was obvious to Ross, Cody and Shorty that Eddy had hurt her so bad, so deep, she'd either die or get better. Or maybe she'd just die and keep living, which was the real danger. If that happened, in spite of everything, they would miss the old Hackenbush very much, because the new one would be way too painful to be around. But whatever was going to happen, what they were wondering at the moment was how long she could last on strictly tequila.

Hackenbush wasn't wondering about anything but getting and staying numb, which meant maintaining a balance of booze and consciousness. To do this, she had to add a few drugs to her regimen. She'd ordered in a gram of blow to keep her upright, more or less, and some dope to help with the nausea. If she passed out for too long, she woke up sober enough to feel pain. It was the same if she lost valuable ounces of tequila from throwing up. Or so she told herself; by then, she'd do anything to alter her emotional and physical state.

Well, almost anything. Mrs. Parker's "Resume" kept running through her head and she was too fucked up to think of any better way to check out.

Damn Eddy Lee anyway, if he was still around... well, maybe she'd be inspired to take him with her. Or just beg him to come back to her.

Anything. Anything but this.

And then the goddamn phone rang, again; probably one of her friends calling to see if she was okay. Ross, Cody and

Shorty had come by at different times with food or more booze or to take away her car keys or simply to call the wagon if she was dead. She didn't care; they cared enough for all of them so there was no need for her to care.

She let the machine pick up. It was Anna Kodaly from Solutionations again, asking her if she was available for a temp assignment, another one had come up, and could she call her back even if she wasn't? Well, fuck, it was nice of Anna to think of her and she'd call back someday and just say no. There was no way in her present condition she could face the Gas Company lifers, even though those gigs paid eleven bucks an hour because she could do Displaywrite and Microsoft Word for PC. Nor could she put on pantyhose and schlep herself to the back office of some commercial enterprise and pay their fucking bills for eight hours a day. She couldn't even get off the couch, for God's sake; how was she supposed to go out there and represent herself as one of the "temporary staffing winners" from Temp Solutionations, as their orientation videos instructed their temps to do? Fuck 'em. Solutionations would have to live without her and vice versa.

Been awhile since she'd seriously temped; just a few days, here and there. That last Solutionations job she'd done as a favor to Val had been a cakewalk, though it seemed like it happened a lifetime ago. Of course this could also be the effect of the long bender she'd been on, so long, in fact, she was no longer sure how long she'd been on it. But, also in another lifetime, *Dr. Hackenbush and her Orchestra* had been enough in demand that she could scrape by on singing without having to temp to make ends meet. Too bad; now she figured the last thing she ever wanted to do was sing again. She'd rather temp or die or have another drink; the last option was, at the moment, the easiest to fulfill, and therefore irresistible.

Hackenbush heard the key turn and thought wildly that Eddy had come back. He was the only other person who had a key to her place. Just opening an eye made her dizzy, so she made no move to get up off the floor.

Person? Well it wasn't exactly a person: it was her landlord. She curled back into fetal position around her bottle. Part of her brain registered that the snort and weed were in the bedroom, where, logically, the Landlord would not go, ha ha. She heard him taking a little tour of his rental and then come back to stand over her for a moment before sitting on the couch.

"It's the sixth, Hackenbush," he said, as if he found all his tenants curled up on the floor. "I need a check or you get this three day notice." He slipped it under her elbow, where she could see it. "Now, if you're a little short on the money side, maybe I could help you out. Y'know? A little barter exchange, just between the two of us."

Hackenbush sat up and looked the leering little bastard in the eye. She found her purse, extracted her checkbook, wrote him a check and told him to get out.

"Let me know if you ever change your mind, Hackenbush," he said on his way out.

'Yeah, we'll go snow-shoeing in hell,' she thought, curling back around her bottle again and trying to re-achieve that state of perfect numbness. But something was tugging at her mind; something numerical. She dragged her checkbook under her eyes, she forced herself to focus on the register. After deducting her rent check, she had twelve dollars and sixty-seven cents to her name. She could gas up the bug and buy a carton of cigarettes. Maybe.

"Can you lend us a secretary from your department for six weeks?" Dr. Brazil asked.

"'Fraid not. How about a temp?"

"Mrs. Azbury, I hardly have money for cell lines or assays, let alone–"

"Different budget item, Doctor. Shall I get you and Dr. Albany a temp or not?"

"Yes, please, and thank you, Mrs. Azbury."

"Oh! It's you!"

"It usually is the person you're calling who picks up the phone, Anna, yes; it is I," Hackenbush said, amused and exhausted, but upright and relatively sober for the first time in, well, she couldn't exactly remember. No booze, a night of sleep, a steamy shower, hot black coffee, and simply being young had worked a miraculous recovery in Hackenbush. Her recent financial crisis had been highly motivational, too. "How are you, darlin'?"

"Fine, just fine. I have a job for you if you can do it."

Hackenbush went through the temp secretary questions:

"Where?" Less than thirty minute commute, which was her limit.

"When?" Starting tomorrow, which was good since she'd been horrified by the hag she'd seen in the mirror that morning.

"How long?" Six weeks was fine. It was hot that July and she usually tried to get a temp job for the summer since it was nice to be in air conditioning most of the day. And besides, she'd probably never sing again, so who cared how long the assignment was.

"How much?" Hmmmm. "That's all?" Well, it would do. "Tell them, I'll be there in the morning. Is the parking free?" It should be in that part of town. "Well, that's good."

"I've heard you're not, ah, doing too well these days, Mabel," Anna said.

"Listening to gossip, are you, Ms. Kodaly?"

"The word gets around, Dr. Hackenbush," Anna said seriously. "I've been calling other people with the jobs you've been ignoring and they told me about Eddy Lee. Sorry, Mabel; he's a crazy man to leave you."

Hackenbush sighed; everything hurt nowadays, even sisterly sympathy. "Thanks, Anna. You know how it is: some days chicken salad; some days chicken shit."

Anna said she'd write that down and said good-bye.

Hackenbush surveyed the wreck of her apartment; wrapped the weed in a baggie to keep it fresh and finished up the blow, which would not keep. She called Cody to get her fucking car keys and a small loan so she could go grocery shopping.

Dr. Albany didn't know exactly when he'd fallen in love with Dr. Brazil. One day he just realized it was a fact, like any other fact in his life.

Too bad for Albany; Brazil was either straight or so far in the closet it was moot anyway. So Albany contented himself with his unrequited love, which, in these immunologically-troubled times, was probably the safest course. Not promiscuous or even bold by nature, Albany was not about to pursue, let alone pressure, Brazil. Unless he could figure out how to do it without destroying their professional relationship or their polite and immaculate friendship.

On the other hand, one didn't get a Ph.D. in virology without being able to see a few clues when they surfaced. Every now and then, Albany detected a kind of yielding in Brazil, a sadness that softened his usually stern fellow researcher. Not wishing to pry or frighten the other man, Albany would simply take advantage of being able to stand a little closer to him and feel an incipient bond reaching, stretching, yearning between them. He was standing very close to Dr. Brazil when an exhausted-looking brunette wearing big, black horn-rimmed glasses thrust open the office door. She looked at them, she looked at the room number, she looked at them again, closed the door in front of her, and knocked on it.

Dr. Brazil took a giant step away from Dr. Albany and opened the door for Dr. Hackenbush.

'What a grubby little joint this is,' Hackenbush thought as she cruised the hallway looking for room forty-four. She found it and, pushing the door open, found two guys who looked like they were about to jump each other. 'Can this possibly be the right room?' she wondered, double-checking the number. Right room; wrong moment (obviously)—try again. She closed the door and knocked on it.

The taller, thinner, blonder guy opened it and waved her in. "Are you our temp? Maria Housenberg?" he asked, consulting a pink phone message.

Hackenbush said she was probably their temp, but she was not now nor had she ever been Maria Housenberg and introduced herself. If they wanted to call the office and check, she'd dial it up for them.

"Those names are, ah, rather similar. I'm sure you're our temp... Mabel? Was it?" He introduced himself as Dr. Brazil and the other guy as Dr. Albany.

"Oh, great! A pair 'o docs," she said, smiling at her own joke.

"I beg your pardon?" Brazil asked, while Albany laughed politely in the background.

"Two doctors," Hackenbush said, deciding that she probably wouldn't share her professional name with this guy since he was humor-deficient; she could tell already. "Let's see, doc; the agency said it was word processing, phones and a little bookkeeping. This my desk?" She waved at the metal hulk near the door. She turned on the computer when they nodded. "Ah, WordStar," she muttered, staring at the screen. "Good to see you again, WordStar."

The phone rang and Brazil answered, "Department twenty-six." He listened and then handed it to Hackenbush.

It was Anna, checking to see if she'd found her way though the maze at the medical school. "Anna! I've told you never to call me here!" Hackenbush said mock-seriously. "Of course I found it. Was I not here when you called?"

Hackenbush assumed Dr. Albany excused himself to go laugh since he was having a tough time keeping a straight face. Dr. Brazil gave her a quick overview of the job and a sheaf of papers to word process. They were for a research grant, just type them in and he'd rearrange them as needed.

Standard stuff for Hackenbush and she set to work. Except for answering the phone or greeting the rare visitor, she was able to focus totally on the job at hand and not be annoyed by any memories. For the most part, she was even able to ignore the residual aches and pains of her binge.

Typing away, she learned that Albany was a Ph.D. and Brazil was an M.D., specifically an oncologist specializing in blood and immune system cancers. Their CVs told her that Albany's education and research were with viruses; at least that was one of the words she could understand in his list of publications. Brazil's papers dealt more with leukemia therapy in the early part of his career, but in the last four years the focus had shifted toward lymphoma, whatever that was.

Usually Hackenbush let this kind of information bounce off her conk. No need to fill up her head with useless data when all she cared about was music. But she took all this in because it kept the noise level in the head way up and those sad, recent memories shut out. Efficient, accurate and swift; Hackenbush typed up the circled text and wondered what kind of a grant they were applying for.

"How are your memoirs coming, Monty?" Alan asked. He was pleased his lover felt well enough to have breakfast with him. Most mornings Monty stayed in bed until after he'd left for the lab.

"Oh, fine, darling, just fine." Monty smiled across his coffee. "Still awash in memories right now; I'll begin sorting them very soon. I think I'll organize them by each show and then intersperse flashbacks to my childhood—the genus of my genius."

Alan merely smiled; he was used to this kind of stagy patter.

"How's Inez? Pop out her kid yet?" Monty asked, shifting his eggs around, but not actually eating them.

"As a matter of fact she did some time ago," Alan said, taking his dishes into the kitchen. "We have a temp; strange girl named Mabel Hackenbush is with us," he added when he came back.

"Dr. Hackenbush?"

"Oh, I don't think she's a doctor, Monty," Alan said, picking up his briefcase. "She's a temp."

"Ask her."

"I was wondering, Mabel, someone I know asked if you were a doctor," Dr. Brazil said later that morning.

"I'm not, but I'm known around town as Dr. Hackenbush formerly of Dr. Hackenbush and her Orchestra," she said, laying even odds on what the next question would be.

"Why?"

'Ah, the scientific mind at its best,' she thought, but said, "When I was a little girl I saw *Day at the Races*, and in that one, Groucho is a vet named Dr. Hugo Hackenbush. I thought that was so great; so I, all of five years old, announced to my father that I, too, would be a vet named Dr. Hackenbush."

"And did you become a vet?"

"No, I became a musician instead, but the name stuck and it's a good hook for the band. Dr. Hackenbush and her

Orchestra is memorable for some reason," she said.

"Oh," he said and handed her a stack of forms to type for the grant submission.

Polite as ever, Hackenbush waited until he was out of earshot to laugh. Well, chuckle really; six clean and sober weeks later she still wasn't laughing much about anything.

She liked this temp gig. It was fairly close to home so she avoided most of the Olympics traffic, and busy enough to keep her thinking about the work in front of her and not the recent past. In the evenings she read with intense concentration and went to bed early. When her financial situation stabilized, she went to the last-run movie theater near Sunset Junction. She hung out with Shorty now and then; he'd play backgammon or rummy and not press her about anything. Ross and Cody called a few times about gigs but just got snarled at for their trouble. One of those gigs was an evening-length theater show in October that they wanted to do very badly. Hackenbush listened to their messages about it and tamped down any incipient interest. She told them to find someone else; they said they'd think about it, the main problem being that Shorty was disinclined to dance with anyone else. "Is this Shorty's gig or ours?" she had asked.

"Well, the deal is for Dr. Hackenbush and her Orchestra," Ross told her. "That includes Shorty and there's money for some horns, too."

"And am I, via Shorty, holding the whole parade up?" she asked.

"Basically, yes."

"Shit." She lit a Pall Mall and picked a piece of tobacco off her tongue. "Any thoughts on where we can rehearse? No room here and I'm too broke to rent anything."

Ross said he'd work on it and the next day dropped off a bundle of music for her to arrange. Thus, in the last weeks of her temp job, Hackenbush was planning an evening length show for October that she really couldn't care less about.

She still had not picked up her baritone ukulele or sung a note since Eddy left her. And so far no one had been able to find a place for them to rehearse, but she figured she'd work that out in September.

So, now it was almost September and her temp job was

ending. She called Anna to tell her when she'd be available again and Anna told her she'd keep it in mind. Evidently firms didn't bother to call the temp agency that much in advance, or they didn't call Temp Solutionations in advance; knowing that in this economy there were scores of hungry, competent temps out there, like Hackenbush, snapping up whatever jobs came along.

"Dr. Hackenbush is working for you?"

"Mabel Hackenbush is working for me, yes," Alan corrected his lover.

Monty ignored it, the way he'd been ignoring Alan's persnickety comments all these years. "What does she do for you all day?"

"She types, she answers phones, she reconciles the petty cash, orders supplies for us, she even took some dictation the other day."

"Shorthand?"

"Steno Script."

One of those telepathic moments between couples of longstanding occurred.

"I'll ask her, Monty, I'll ask her."

"Mabel, do you ever take private secretary jobs?" Brazil asked.

"Depends on the job," she said, thinking she really needed one for next Monday, private or otherwise. She proceeded through the standard where-how much-how long questions and they soon agreed on an hourly rate. The job would start Monday, last for a week and then they would see if they all wanted another week.

"The person you'll be working with hasn't been well for some time," Brazil said blandly. "I hope that won't cause a problem."

"Is it contagious?"

"No, not really."

"What do you mean 'not really'?" Mabel watched him fidget and thought men with advanced degrees should not fidget, even though it was kind of cute.

"It's not something you could easily catch," Brazil said,

watching her face.

"How so?"

"It's sexually transmitted."

"AIDS?" she asked, knowing that everything else got cured or hidden. He nodded; she nodded back. "Well, as long as you're not hiring me to have sex with him, I suppose we'll be fine. I know some people that know some people who have it; it's a big downer."

"Yes. Very."

On Hackenbush's last day, Dr. Albany took her to lunch at a fish taco place near the lab.

Since the day she arrived, she'd been discreetly on the lookout for any further signs of passion between Albany and Brazil. Her attention was unrewarded as they were the very models of self-control, at least when she was around.

Well, that was okay; Hackenbush was through with love and even watching other people thrash around in it would soon no longer be interesting. She'd excise it from her roster of enjoyable experiences until she was old enough not to care how other people lacerated themselves. With luck, she'd be one of those little old ladies that enjoy watching other people's marriages disintegrate. Good to know there was something to look forward to.

But right now, sitting across from Albany, whom she liked as a boss, she couldn't help but wonder why this half of the closet case love affair wasn't with someone else. He was attractive in a dark hair and broad shoulders kind of way; he was a doctor; he was gainfully employed; he had nice gray eyes; he did not, as far as she knew, play the guitar or mainline heroin; seemed like some nice young man would have snapped him up years ago. He had a light drawl and slow, almost hesitant way of speaking when he spoke, which was seldom and only when spoken to. Great listeners are rare, but Hackenbush suspected Albany might fade into the wallpaper a little too easily for the right guy to notice him. On the other hand, it seemed like Albany was always at the lab, so as far as Hackenbush knew, he wasn't even getting out where he could be noticed. As she recalled, dating was hard enough but impossible if you never got out there to do it.

And, she reckoned, if he was in love with Brazil, it was convenient that he never had time to find someone else. Of course being in love with that iceberg Brazil was like a vow of celibacy. And perhaps that was for the best in these infectious times. After all, science hadn't cured herpes yet, let alone the AIDS thing and even the various types of clap that could be cured were hell on the body. More and more, celibacy was looking to Hackenbush like the only way to fly.

She was through with love (which meant sex too, since she was never cold-blooded enough to enjoy pure technique) and had better things to think about than other people's romances.

"So... where are you off to on Monday?" Albany asked when Hackenbush stared at him until he was forced to hold up his end of their lunchtime conversation.

"Private secretary job up in South Pas," she said, thinking that if Brazil wanted Albany to know he'd hired her, he would have told him already. Not that Brazil's privacy was all that important, but he was her employer now and she thought it might be best not to offend him.

"I hope we didn't torture you too much, Mabel," he said, almost shyly.

"Oh, it was fine; it's not your fault the grant guidelines are written by sociopaths." She smiled when he smiled at her joke. Of the two, Albany had the more developed sense of humor. "Dr. Brazil is a little, ah, intense."

"Well... you'll have to excuse him," Albany said, collecting their paper plates. "Alan's an oncologist; he sees most of his patients die because the cures don't exist yet. So... he does everything he can, but, there's only so much you can do for leukemia and most of the lymphomas–"

"What is that?" Hackenbush asked, figuring she could learn one more thing on her last day. "Lymphoma, I mean."

"Cancer of the lymph or immune system," Albany said. "So... about Alan, a job like his, it does something to people; at the very least it makes them intense. That's why I decided not to get an M.D.; I like people, but I'd rather not deal directly with their diseases."

"I can dig it." She followed him to his car. "I hope you get your grant," she said when they were on their way.

"Me, too. I've no idea why, but there's not much money out there to study this new disease," he said. "If we knew more about it, it... it could, in some ways, resemble a communicable lymph cancer and the communicable cancer part of it should be scaring the hell out of everyone, but nobody seems to care much. But... it's not in the general population." He downshifted to a stop and looked over at her. "Yet," he added.

Driving home that afternoon, Hackenbush stopped at a light and watched a guy with purple spots all over his face cross the street in front of her. He was in rags, muttering and pushing a shopping cart. From the signs, Hackenbush assumed he was homeless and wondered how a person like that gets any care when they're that sick. She further wondered how he got it and what he was doing with it.

The light changed and she drove on.

Over the weekend, an Asian driver cut her off on the freeway. In her offhand way, Hackenbush wished AIDS had struck the Asian driver population. If it had, by now, not only would science know the cause, they'd have a cure and a vaccine on the market. Only a handful of people would have gotten sick and the first Asian-American native son would be running for president of the United States. And if he or she was running as a Democrat, Mabel Hackenbush would not only vote, but campaign for him or her.

But mostly that weekend, she stayed home and worked on arrangements. They were all songs she knew, except "Good Morning, Heartache", which was new to her. She might have ventured to the Brand Library for a recording had it not been astonishingly hot that weekend. The air-cooled VW engine was a wonderful thing, but Mabel tried not to push her luck in hot weather.

This September might not have been any hotter than the others, but seemed worse because she had to keep her windows locked at night. There was a serial killer on the loose, most recently in Glendale, which was not far from her apartment in Echo Park. At least Hackenbush thought that was too close for comfort. So the windows stayed locked and the fan stayed on, for all the good it did moving the hot and stuffy air around her little place.

She had to be extra careful not to smear the drying ink with her sweaty forearm as she copied parts for the arrangements.

At nine sharp on Monday, Hackenbush arrived at the address Dr. Brazil gave her. It turned out not to be South Pasadena, as she'd thought, but South Pasadena adjacent. Could have fooled Hackenbush; the quiet street and large house set back from it simply screamed South Pasadena to her. Perhaps these were distinctions for others to make; for Hackenbush, well, she was there to make some money.

She was slightly startled when Dr. Brazil opened the door for her and ushered her into a big room with hardwood floors and sunny windows. He introduced her to Monty Vista, of whom she'd heard.

"Not the Monty Vista? The director-choreographer-dancer-actor and all around bon vivant Monty Vista?" Hackenbush asked.

"The very same," he said, waving her to a chair. "Please excuse the purple spots."

"Oh, not to worry; all the best people are wearing them this year," she said turning the charm up a notch.

"How kind of you, Dr. Hackenbush. Alas, the worst part is that this is just not my color at all."

In perfect rhythm, they laughed annoyingly stagy laughs. The kind you hear in the lobby, between acts of incomprehensible music-drama events. Hackenbush glanced at Brazil, who looked completely horrified, and then she got another mild shock.

"Darling, I'm sure we'll be fine." Monty smiled up at the doctor. "You're leaving me in Hackenbush's capable hands, so run along to work; I'm sure you're being missed."

It was a dismissal, however suave, but a dismissal nevertheless. Dr. Brazil jibbed ever so slightly by reminding Hackenbush where she could find him if she needed to and by pointing out the steno pad and pens on the table in front of her. Much to Hackenbush's relief, he finally left before Monty could get really bitchy.

"Now, Mr. Vista," Hackenbush said, opening a pad and

poising a pen. "Where shall we begin?"

"You know, Hackenbush, I'm rather thirsty. Would you mind terribly manning the blender?"

"I'd be delighted."

"Excellent; ever had a Ramos Gin Fizz?"

"No, never heard of it," Hackenbush said. "I'm not much of a gin drinker."

"Not a gin drinker, my dear little savage? This is like an Orange Julius with gin."

"Ah," she said, thinking that she liked Orange Juliuses, at least the ones her father bought her at the South Coast Plaza mall long ago. She would soon find out that she liked Ramos Gin Fizzes very much, too, even though they were a pain in the ass to make.

> 1-1/2 ounces gin
>
> 2 or 3 drops orange flower water
>
> 2 egg whites
>
> 1 tablespoon of powered sugar
>
> 1/2 teaspoon lemon juice
>
> 2 ounces half and half or whipping cream
>
> 1or two drops vanilla extract
>
> 1/2 cup ice coarsely cracked

At his request, Hackenbush brought all the ingredients and the blender to the table. With Monty coaching, Hackenbush carefully separated the white from the yolk and dropped it with the other stuff in the blender. "Contact." She flipped the blender on high and shut if off at Monty's command.

They drank; it was one of the best things she'd ever had in her life.

"My dear, you look positively euphoric," Monty said, smiling over his drink.

"You know, Mr. Vista—"

"Monty, my dear Hackenbush, Monty."

"You know, Monty, this is better than an Orange Julius; less sweet and more creamy."

"It's the gin, Hackenbush; makes life less saccharine and more creamy as only good gin can," Monty said, suggesting another round.

Drinking Gin Fizzes is not the fastest way to get

smashed, but will certainly get one there eventually. And the ride is pretty nice, too. Yes, they did get some work done; they made an outline for Monty's memoirs based on his shows. Hackenbush took down some libelous stories that she was instructed to read back and then burn, which she did in the ashtray. At one point, Monty asked her to go into his bedroom and get his cigarette holder from the back of the bottom drawer of the bureau in the closet.

"I'm not supposed to smoke," he said, fitting one of Hackenbush's Pall Malls into the holder. "But you're the first smoker I've had around in months and what possible difference can it make now?"

"Hmmmm, well, every little bit helps I suppose," she said vaguely.

"You sound like Alan," Monty said, puffing away. "It's easy to be optimistic for others, Hackenbush."

"Sorry. Want me to see if I can score some heroin or anti-freeze for you?"

"Not yet, Hackenbush, not yet." Monty laughed at her. "You can tell me what you think of Alan though."

"Dr. Brazil?"

"Oh, call him Alan; Dr. Brazil sounds like a rum drink."

"He seems like a nice guy, a little on the uptight side, but he's a doctor, after all."

"Yes, he's terribly nice," Monty agreed. "Rather on the passive-aggressive side, but very nice about it. Quite apologetic on occasion."

"I just worked for him for a few weeks."

"But can you see him with a lover?"

Hackenbush frowned over this idea for a few minutes and then admitted that, no, she couldn't. "I can't even see him with his lab coat off," she said.

Monty studied her for a moment and then suggested she whip up another round. "And put some gin in it this time."

There were several more pages of unprintable reminiscences to be burned before Monty asked, apropos of very little, "Have you been in love, Hackenbush?"

Hackenbush studied him over her steno pad for two beats before she answered, "Yeah, once."

"You don't sound very enthusiastic."

"It was fun while it lasted," she said. "But it hardly seems worth the pain now."

"I take it this is a fresh wound?"

"Late last spring."

"My dear, I am so sorry," Monty said. "But you're only in pain because you haven't found a new love."

"It's not that simple, I–"

"No, not for you, Hackenbush," he said. "Hear me out. If you'd found a new love before your lover dumped you, wouldn't you be happy?"

"What?"

"Yes, as I suspected," Monty went on. "I've known what I must do for quite a while now, but the help I've needed has never materialized. Hackenbush, I need you."

"I'm here to work on your book." She waved her steno pad at him.

"I need you," he said, staring into her eyes, "to help me find a new lover for Alan Brazil."

"I am here," she said staring back at him, "to work on your book."

"Hackenbush, if you could alleviate a little suffering in the world, would you do it?" he asked.

"Maybe."

Monty took a deep breath. "I'm the only lover Alan has ever had," he said quietly. "And I've been completely unworthy of him." He paused for only as long as it took Hackenbush to make another blender to Gin Fizzes. They drank, and Monty recounted meeting a very young med student named Brazil at a party, wooing and winning him, and then growing tired of him. He sent her into his bedroom to get the photo on the dressing table.

"But I was all poor Alan had," Monty said tragically, gazing at a very young and callow Alan Brazil. "Well, he had a medical degree and a hospital job, but that was it."

Apparently, the unhappy couple stayed together through Monty's philandering and carrying on with everything male with a pulse. They presented a happy, successful gay couple to the world, when in truth, they hardly saw each other at home. This gave Monty an excuse to never commit to a new lover and Alan an excuse to be miserable, but not miserable enough to find someone else.

"And then I got sick, and Alan has been a saint to me," Monty said. "We need another round, dear, and put some gin in–"

"Yeah yeah yeah." Hackenbush put a lot of gin in it and drank up while Monty continued.

"So, I look at you, Hackenbush, in your suffering because you've loved and, I assume, lost, and I vividly and graphically see what Alan's suffering will be when I leave this mortal coil, and I wish, at all costs to avoid that for him," Monty said. "I have long suspected that if I don't find him a lover before I go, he will never recover from his love for me, and I could not stand that kind of future."

Hackenbush was having a little trouble standing the present. "Won't you be dead?" she asked, with as much tact as the gin would allow.

"It won't matter."

"And are you sure he loves you as much as you think?" she asked. "It sounds like you've been a total prick to him for years."

"Of course he loves me, Hackenbush, he doesn't know any better," Monty snapped. "I must find him a new lover. And that's where you come in."

"Me? He's queer, what would he want with me?" Hackenbush ignored the blender and just dumped a couple of fingers of gin in each glass.

"Nothing," Monty said after a few sips. "I want you to help me find him someone. I've exhausted all the eligible men I know. As you can imagine, Alan doesn't enjoy the company of flamboyant men other than myself. I'm really enough for several men. But I digress. You, Hackenbush, you're out and about, you must know a gay man who'd be right for Alan."

"I'm not much of a fag hag, Monty," she said, taking Shorty right off the list of eligible homosexuals. "But I think I might be able to help you," she said, and briefly sketched out the Albany-Brazil non-romance.

"He sounds like the perfect man!" Monty rubbed his hands together.

"Alan's never mentioned him to you?"

"No, but Alan's more a listener than talker," Monty said.

"I bet," Hackenbush said, figuring Alan probably gave up trying to get a word in edgewise long ago. "So what now?" she asked. "Oh, and we're out of gin."

"See if you can get some lime juice, too; these fizzes aren't citrusy enough."

"Dig it. Why don't you go take a quick nap while I see if I can get Nathan to stop at the liquor store on the way here?" she asked, and then patted his hand when he tried to get up. "Hold tight, darlin', I got a better way." She staggered into the bedroom and came out with a wheelchair. "I saw this when I was looking for the picture," she said, wheeling it up and helping him into it. She got him into bed and went to call Dr. Albany.

Hackenbush's luck must have been changing because Nathan Albany, the perfect man himself, answered the phone.

Probably the last person Nathan expected to hear from that afternoon was Hackenbush.

In many ways it was refreshing to hear her rather slurred tones. Inez was back on the job as usual and was complaining that "the temp" hadn't done a laundry list of tasks. Albany was too polite to point out that those were things Inez should have done before she left, so he didn't. He knew Alan would do it if Inez kept whining about it. So now she was pouting instead of whining, which was at least quieter.

"Hackenbush!" Happy as he was, Albany kept his voice low. There was something illicit about this call. 'The other woman; the temp,' he thought. "Nice to hear from you, where–?"

"I'm calling on urgent business, Dr. Albany. You, and only you, can help me."

"Hackenbush? What the–?"

"In fact, it concerns you and Dr. Brazil. And urgently concerns you and Dr. Brazil."

'Oh Lord, Hackenbush, what have you done?' he wondered. His mind flew to the controlled drugs, syringes and whatnot in the lab. She couldn't have... "So... what kind of, ah, trouble are you in, Mabel?"

"Well, none. Yet. Can you get away and meet me? As

I said, it's urgent."

Albany glanced at his watch. It was late enough in the day that he could leave without arousing much suspicion. He hated to admit it, but Hackenbush intrigued him and he figured he could handle whatever she tossed his way. "I shouldn't... But..."

"It's urgent."

"...but if it's urgent," he said, pulling a pad toward him. "When and where?" He wrote the address, telephone and directions she gave him and paused. "How much gin? I don't think it's sold by the gallon... okay, two fifths then. And lime juice. And eggs. Hackenbush, are you sure...? Okay, okay; I'll urgently go to the store and be there as soon as I can."

Hackenbush leaned back and lit a victory cigarette. For the first time in a long time, she almost wished she had her ukulele to amuse herself with until the good doctor arrived, but she did not, so she amused herself by cleaning up the Vista-Hackenbush Ramos Gin Fizz mill.

A messy drink, but worth it, even though dried egg whites are hell to scrub off glass. Eventually she had the blender in an acceptable condition and left everything, including the ashtray, in the dish drainer. She opened a window and turned on a fan to get some new air circulating. It was a hot day, so the air that came in was also hot, but still fresher than the smoky ozone they'd been breathing.

It was a nice big room; the band would fit in it with room to dance with Shorty, too.

She peeked at Monty, who was sleeping peacefully. She found some aspirin in the bathroom and took a pair as a prophylactic, figuring there would be more drinking when the gin arrived.

If it arrived. She couldn't believe her luck and thanked the benevolent stars that Albany didn't put up much of a struggle. Hackenbush would have told anyone who called her with a nutty story like that to go to hell. Or maybe Albany was just the trusting sort and really should pair off with Brazil, who would never have let him go on such a wild errand.

Of course if he did end up with Brazil, there would be

no more wild errands, so it was moot.

She got her bag and found a mirror. 'Must be those nutritious egg whites,' she thought, checking the damage, which was minimal. But it was early yet. She brushed her hair and put on some lip gloss. Her shaggy brown mop needed a trim, but only she and her hairdresser could see that. In a week the world would see it, so she had better go soon.

Monty's record collection—she assumed it was his—impressed her. He had the same Coltrane records she did and the Nina Simone album, *Jazz As Played In An Exclusive Side Street Club,* she adored. There was late Billie Holiday, which Hackenbush would loathe until she was old enough to appreciate the phrasing and sentiment behind that destroyed voice. Ella and Sarah, whom she did not like: Ella because the sheer beauty of her voice overpowered the material and Hackenbush thought her scatting was way too desperate. Sarah had a voice that went right through you, like a saber, so that was no fun either. A hard voice; no warmth, no irony, no humor; nothing in it to cheer a sad woman or make a careless one think twice about.

But Billie Holiday of the 1930s and 40s had it all. The quality of her voice was not intimidating and she didn't use it to attack her listeners. Her singing went in and warmed you, made you a co-conspirator in the big, usually ugly, joke of life. There was cheer in Holiday's singing, maybe not for herself, but for the listener. There was a resigned shrug and a sisterly pat on the shoulder; as if to say "oh well, this song will end, but life goes on; you might as well live."

And then in the 50s it was too late and her life didn't go on much longer. She still sang and left a few records from those years that made Hackenbush wince. Miles Davis said Billie was better at the end, but Hackenbush couldn't see it that way. And, being more of a Coltrane fan, she thought Miles was wrong about a lot of things. However, for Billie Holiday, for one short life, since that was all she got, well, she sure did a lot with it.

Hackenbush made a mental note of the location of the records she might want to listen to later. She pulled the sleeves out an inch so she could find them even faster.

She was just finishing that up, when she heard the toilet

flush. A disheveled Monty came in and looked at her like he'd never seen her before. It was only a moment before he pulled himself together but his blank stare chilled her to the marrow. "Not yet," she said.

"How long?"

"If he doesn't get lost, I'd say another fifteen minutes," she said. "How about you go put some rouge on?"

"Really, Hackenbush." However, he did go back into the bedroom and returned all brushed and tidy. "And how did you lure him here, my siren?"

"I said it was urgent. And as I fascinate all men, he decided to find out how urgent," she said, joining him at the dining table. "I also dropped Alan's name and that seemed to have some effect."

"An excellent sign."

"Well, I thought so." The doorbell rang. "But, lo! Can this be our likely guy?" She sprang up.

"Don't be too eager, Hackenbush, and I'll do the talking," Monty said, fitting one of her cigarettes into his holder.

Very politely, Hackenbush opened the door and took one of the bags off Dr. Albany's hands. "Did you get the lime juice?" she asked.

Albany nodded but didn't say anything; he was too busy looking Monty over as they crossed the room.

"Hackenbush." Monty waved them impatiently forward. "Introductions."

"Monty, please meet Dr. Nathan Albany. Dr. Albany, please meet Mr. Monty Vista," Hackenbush rapped out. She was a gal who knew her way around introducing people. "How much lime juice?" she asked Monty.

"Half teaspoon."

"I'll be in the kitchen with the blender," she said, picked up the grocery bags and went there.

"Good lass. Please sit down, Dr. Albany; over here, on my right where you'll have a better view of my purple spots. I understand you work with Alan," Monty said graciously and directed him to a chair.

"Dr. Brazil?"

"And none other. May I call you Nathan?"

"Please. So... Mr. Vista..."

"Monty, Nathan, Monty. That's what Alan calls me. He used to howl it in ecstasy, but those days, alas, are over for us now. Actually have been for quite awhile." He inclined his head at the sound of the blender. "Ah, what a delightful sound."

"About Dr. Brazil..."

"Call him Alan," Monty said sternly. "I do."

"About Alan..."

Although Hackenbush was a failed waitress, she was capable of carrying three large drinks to Monty's table and did so with much élan.

"Ah, my dear Hackenbush; do join us." Monty tried his drink and said it was perfect. "I believe you and Alan have had the pleasure of this lovely creature's company for the past few weeks, have you not, Nathan?"

"Ah.. yes..."

"Lucky you! So far she's proved her worth as a drinks mixer and matchmaker," Monty said suavely. "She tells me sparks fly between you and Alan, but sadly no flame. Yet." He exchanged arch looks with Hackenbush that would have been played for the top balcony at the Dorothy Chandler Pavilion.

Nathan had the grace to blush. "Look... Hackenbush, I think you misunderstood what you walked in on that first day. You–"

"Nonsense, Nathan, nonsense!" Monty cut him off. "Here you have a female who, for a variety of rather stupid reasons, is through with love, or so she tells me, but can still spot the symptoms in others. Not unlike a newly sober drunk seeing drunkenness in others with a mixture of envy and repulsion. Such sensibilities are rare in modern women, who seem always to be running thither and yon, from man to man to man to man to man to man, in an endless quest for validation of their utterly useless, pointless and puerile existence. But here you have Hackenbush! A woman among women; a woman who recognizes as fact the utter futility of existence in general and resistance to doing my bidding in particular, and very nicely, too. After all, dear man, here you are! But you don't seem to be drinking your drink. Not a gin lover? Shall Hackenbush get you something else? Such a bonus for her to be useful as well as decorative. So few women are, you know. What shall we switch to? Gimlets, Martinis, Old Fashioneds?"

"Ah... no thanks, I–"

"Screwdrivers?" Monty asked.

There was silence while Nathan tasted his drink. "So... What is this?" he asked, licking his lips.

"A Ramos Gin Fizz," Monty said. "The Orange Julius of the gin drinks family." And then he sat back and got the relaxed and thoughtful host look on his face. This also allowed him to conserve a little energy while he waited for Nathan to either ask the right question or bolt from the room.

Dr. Albany could wait a little, too. He looked at Hackenbush, who simply smiled her professional temp secretary smile at him. No help there.

Nathan Albany had spent most of his life dealing with mute microscopic creatures that, fascinating as they were, were not much in the way of conversation. He'd never felt comfortable with smooth talkers like Monty Vista and, were Hackenbush not there, would have left by now. This Vista character was everything his mother had ever warned him about. She had warned him about flamboyant, arrogant and charming (i.e. scheming, to use her word) women. Possibly this was why he'd become homosexual, to avoid those kind of women. Nevertheless, his mother's warning could very well apply to Monty Vista.

Hackenbush had seemed like such a level-headed girl in the office, yet she had lured him here to meet this man. Of course how people are in their professional lives is very different from how they are at home. And further—Dr. Albany began a dangerous train of thought—this must be very true of Dr. Brazil if he is on a first name basis with this strange Vista person. So, weighing the difference between leaving later than sooner, Nathan sucked down half his drink and asked the question that would keep him there a while longer. "So... Monty, um, how do you know Alan?"

"Oh, we've only been living together for the past eighteen years," Monty drawled and then watched the doc choke on his drink. "I gather that's come as a surprise to you,

Nathan." He swung his gaze to Hackenbush and asked if she knew the Heimlich maneuver.

"I pureed the ice; what could he be choking on?" she asked.

Monty said, "Ah," and politely waited for the doctor's coughing fit to subside. "I see Alan is as loquacious at work as he is at home because I didn't know a thing about you either, Nathan. You'd think Alan would have mentioned he was working with a tall, dark and handsome doctor at some point in our relationship, if only to make me jealous."

"You have nothing to be jealous about, Monty," Nathan assured him, quickly.

"Yes, dammit, and that's just the problem; Alan is the perfect man," Monty fumed, lighting another of Hackenbush's cigarettes. "Honest, modest, reticent, intelligent, hard working, attractive, faithful, thrifty, scrupulous, tender; all the things another man could appreciate if he wasn't chasing chorus boys and leather punks.

"Actually, chasing other men wasn't really my problem; catching them, that was the problem.

"But I digress, and this isn't about me; it's about Alan. Or rather, it's about me fixing Alan up with some decent male before I die. So, it is about me; nevertheless, since you didn't bolt while you had the chance, it now concerns you, Nathan."

"Oh? How so?" Nathan asked, finishing his drink.

"Well, I'll tell you, but let's have another drink. And due to the late hour, let's switch to martinis," Monty said. "Hackenbush... what's wrong?"

"I had a bad experience with martinis on my twenty-first birthday," she said, wincing.

"Really? Tell us."

"My father took me out for my first legal drink. I like to shoot tequila, still do now and then, and also got the bright idea to keep shooting, but with martini chasers," she said.

"And what happened?" Nathan asked horrified.

"I blacked out so I don't really know. But everyone tells me I'm lucky to be alive."

"Well then, it's high time you got over it and back in the saddle, Hackenbush," Monty said, waving her story away and gave her directions on proper martini making. "What an

45

education you're getting here, my dear," he said watching her deftly clear the table. "At this rate, you'll be nigh on the perfect woman by the end of the week."

"Why don't we shoot for perfection on Wednesday and a graceful decay over the weekend?" Hackenbush asked, returning with glasses, vermouth and a shaker.

"Olives, Hackenbush, olives! What kind of a monster are you?"

"Yours, Monty, all yours."

"Just get the olives, Igor, and shut up."

Hackenbush winked at Albany, who was looking on with in a combination of amusement and alarm. Much to her relief, the doc had obviously decided to stick around for the pitch, whatever it would be by the time Monty got around to it. And whatever it was, it'd be a good show, as she could see Monty warming to his subject quite nicely. "I've always wondered about these," she said, holding up the strainer.

"Fill it with ice," Monty said. "Pour in the gin, but don't splash it on the ice. It's bad for the gin to be bashed around."

"And then?"

He reached over and stirred the ice and gin for a moment. "Hand me the vermouth." She did and he put a few drops in. "Now, without any superfluous movements, pour it through the strainer. And don't forget the olives. Or would you prefer a lemon twist, Nathan?" he asked the doctor.

"Oh... olives," Nathan said, tasting his gin. "I'd hate to break with tradition."

They drank in silence for a while.

"So, Nathan, how long have you worked with Alan?" Monty asked.

"Six years," he said. "But... Hackenbush can tell you we don't work very closely."

"Alas," Monty said. "You might have nailed him by now if you did."

"Oh, I doubt that, Monty. He's not that kind of man." Nathan accepted more martini from Hackenbush. "And... working in the same department, occasionally on the same projects, we have to maintain a professional relationship. And... he's a fine researcher and scientist; I wouldn't want to destroy a good working partnership for a cheap fling. Wouldn't be worth it, would it?"

"You're totally asking the wrong guy, Nathan." Hackenbush could barely speak for laughing.

"Young woman, control yourself or I'll have you banished to the kitchen," Monty said sternly and then turned to Albany. "Theoretically, I agree with you, Nathan, however, I've never let theory interfere with my practice of seduction." He gave Hackenbush a hard look to stop her giggling, which it did. "Gallant and noble sentiments you've expressed here and I can understand, if not appreciate them. Me, I've spent my life getting laid. As you can see, that has proven to be fatal. I accept that. Like it, no; accept it, yes.

"Of course, Alan is different from me. I frankly don't know what he does with his libido and haven't much cared until recently. Recently I began to think of his future; a future without me to stimulate him. Mentally stimulate him; we've merely been housemates for years, if you must know.

"However, this is entirely Alan's fault; he should have tossed me into the street years ago and found someone better or worse. But, no, and here we are in our chaste and pious sham of a marriage, bound as much by guilt as by affection. Leaving all this will be the upside of death; I shall shake off Alan's love with this mortal coil when I leave this vale of tears, Nathan, when I leave this vale of tears."

He paused to scowl at Hackenbush, who'd very obviously looked at her watch. "So, I will be dead but Alan will be very much alive," Monty began again. "And so will you, my dear Nathan, so will you.

"I have asked for the moon and the stars in this life and gotten most of what I've wanted. I'd say I've managed at least ninety-five percent; not bad for one aging, dying fag in Hollywood.

"However, as I am ever closer to glory or oblivion (I'm sure I will find out and be suitably disappointed), I find I have only one desire left in my diseased and decaying body, in my exhausted and resigned mind, in my weary, weary soul. That one desire, one longing, is to see Alan, my Alan, as your Alan, safely ensconced in your bed and your heart. The exact order is not at all important. I then feel I can die in peace, knowing that Alan has a new, and hopefully more rewarding, love and is loved, hopefully better, and the worms can have whatever they want of me and I will go on... to whatever people like me go on to." Looking pious, he sat back and folded his wasted hands in front of him.

"Let me, ah... understand this," Nathan said after a few moments. "You want me to go to bed with Alan. Is that correct?"

"No!" Monty shouted. "I want you to succeed me as the center of his life! But that won't be easy, Nathan, it will be a quest and a challenge and all that heroic romantic bullshit. Your biggest obstacle will be his incredible obtuseness. It's his obtuseness you'll have to overcome. That's Alan, obtuse; knowing that he has an aching void but refusing to see it, own it or fill it. That is your task, Nathan, to fill Alan's aching void!"

"Yeah, well, good luck with that," Hackenbush said sourly and turned to her boss. "Monty, what a bunch of dreck you're talking. Of course you want him to go to bed with Alan, like he said. I mean, how can he become the center of his life or whatever if he doesn't seduce him?"

"Ah... my thought exactly, Hackenbush," Nathan said.

"See, Monty? I tolja dis guy's made t'order," she said.

"Enunciate, Hackenbush, enunciate." Monty scowled at her.

"And that's exactly what I cannot do," Nathan said, trying not to slur his words. "Is seduce Alan; I...I respect him too much."

Hackenbush and Monty exchanged puzzled looks.

"Don't be silly," Hackenbush said tartly. "You can respect him after you seduce him. You can respect him for having the good taste to let you seduce him. You can respect him for finding you attractive enough to let you seduce him. Oh my God, I'm talking my own self into this!"

"Relax, Mabel, relax," Monty said, patting her hand. "Don't forget, you've had a lot to drink and it's not even cocktail time yet." He turned to his other drinking companion. "Now, look here, Nathan; I'm not asking you to do anything you don't, deep inside, want to do. If your morals are bothering you, well, what if you just stand around and wait for Alan to fall into your arms. How would that be?"

"Well... that sounds better," Nathan said, dubiously. "But how can that be accomplished?"

"Leave that to me and La Hackenbush," Monty said and asked La Hackenbush to bring him the phone. "What's the number of Alan's lab, Nathan? I never call there. Thanks," he said when the number was rattled off to him. "Hello, darling," he said into the phone, winking at Hackenbush. "We have a dinner guest tonight so don't linger at work... Never mind who it is; you'll like him... And we'll switch to Gimlets when you get here since you like them so much, so pick up some Rose's Lime Juice on your way home; we're out... Food? Oh, we'll order something in or Hackenbush can scramble some eggs, she's really quite resourceful... Yes, she's still here, slaving away for me... (What's that, Hackenbush? Eggs?) Oh, Alan, and eggs; we're also out of eggs... Yes, Rose's Lime Juice and eggs... See you soon, darling." He hung up the phone and smiled beatifically. "Martinis for all, Hackenbush!"

Dr. Brazil put the phone down and sighed. Another evening of being polite to one of Monty's annoying friends ahead of him after a long day in the lab was almost more than he could bear. But, sadly, he would only have to bear it for just a short while longer. And then he would be alone in the peace and quiet of his orderly life.

But humoring Monty was easier than trying to fight him about anything. And usually, when he finally gave in, Alan ended up enjoying whatever lark Monty wanted him to go on. It had lately become much easier to give in; Monty's health had deteriorated to the point that his whims were minor and therefore manageable. A dinner party would not be overly taxing for Alan since Monty would probably fade out halfway through it.

Before he locked up, he called a few liquor stores to make sure at least one of them had Rose's Lime Juice on hand and to please hold it at the counter for him. It was bad enough he had to run this errand; having to run it several times would merely compound his annoyance. He turned off the lights and computer and left for the day.

At least, if he understood correctly, Hackenbush would be there to help out with the entertaining, which would remove some of the burden from Alan. She seemed like a nice level-headed sort of girl.

At just that moment Hackenbush was dancing to Django Reinhardt's "Lady Be Good" as choreographed by Monty Vista. Having mastered, in her level-headed way, the steps Monty shouted out to her, she was dancing with abandon and something close to joy. Well, closer to joy than she'd been for quite some time. She was also sobering up, which was the whole point.

When she spilled her drink, Monty ordered her to put on the record and dance. "I hate waste," he growled. "Don't you, Nathan?"

The doctor had agreed and taken over the martini-making until Hackenbush could be trusted with it again.

Hackenbush flopped into a chair and lit a cigarette. She smoked moodily and let a couple of songs go by. "How 'bout this one?" she asked Monty.

"'Night And Day'? Well, why not?" Monty sat back, gave her a rough sketch of the steps and then had her start the record over. "On your toes, Hackenbush! You're stomping around like a drunken flamenco dancer!"

"In my dreams!" Hackenbush yelled, striking a flamenco pose and snapping her fingers while still dancing Monty's glorified shuffle until the old bastard had the grace to laugh at her.

After two more repetitions, Monty called her to the table and told her to take a break. "Why aren't you singing, Hackenbush? That's what you do isn't it?" he asked, pouring her a new drink.

"Too hard to sing and dance at the same time," she lied.

"Is zat so?"

"Zat's so," she said with more confidence than she felt. The last thing she wanted to do at that moment was sing. She was still closed up, curled in on herself so she wouldn't feel too much, think too much, remember too much. Her chest felt very tight inside and the leap of faith required to sing... well, maybe tomorrow or the next day. But tonight, no; no singing tonight.

So she was neither singing nor dancing when Dr. Brazil rolled in with the Rose's Lime Juice and eggs. Hackenbush was sitting quietly, watching the look of shock and horror and then surprise and anger go over Alan's usually bland face when he saw Dr. Albany sitting next to Monty.

When he came to a stunned halt half way across the room, Hackenbush sprang into action because she wanted a gimlet and wanted one badly. She glided over and took the bag from him. "Howya wantcher eggs, Monty?"

"Pronounced more clearly, my dear, for a start," Monty said levelly, never taking his eyes off Alan.

"Fine. How would you like to have–"

"So... perhaps I should go," Nathan suggested, his nerve crumbling.

"Nonsense! We're switching to gimlets for Alan's sake and he's just arrived, hasn't he?" Monty waved Hackenbush to his side and took the bottle from her. "Half Rose's Lime Juice and half gin," he said.

"In that order?"

"I'll leave that to you, Hackenbush," he said. "You're coming along so nicely, I feel confident you'll make the right decision." He patted her arm and smiled at her. "Alan, sit down; I think you know everyone."

"I was wondering where you'd got to this afternoon," Alan mumbled at Nathan, taking a seat across the table from him.

"I... hope you don't mind," Nathan said, sipping the green drink Hackenbush handed him. "I can't taste the gin."

"Oh, but it's there, laddie, believe me, it's there." Monty smiled wickedly. "What do you think, Hackenbush?"

"I think I've been wasting my time with tequila all these years."

"How old are you?"

"Twenty-eight."

"Just in the nick of time, my dear!" Monty turned affably to Nathan and asked him what he usually drank.

"I'm usually a vodka drinker," he said, unbending a little. "I find the hangovers are less brutal than whiskey and certainly less than tequila."

"Hmmmm, and I haven't blacked out yet," Hackenbush said. "At least not that I'm aware of."

"Nor that I've noticed, but I wouldn't, would I?" Monty laughed. "Nathan?"

Albany shook his head. "No... I haven't blacked out.. yet."

"Yeah, yeah; what's for dinner?" she asked, pouring another round.

"Thai food?" Monty suggested and smiled at Nathan's nod.

"As long as we can get it delivered," she said, looking around for a phone book. "I might not be blacked out but I do know I'm in zero shape to drive."

Monty smiled and turned to Alan. "What's that place you like? Starts with a P... they deliver, no?"

"Yes; I'll get the menu. Hackenbush can help me." He went into the kitchen, dragging the singer along with him. "What the hell...?" he began, when he saw the empty gin bottles on the counter, he broke off slack jawed.

"Oh! My! God!" Taking her chance to escape, Hackenbush darted back into the big room. "Monty! We're damn near out of gin again! Whatever will become of us?" She flung her arm over her eyes.

"I don't know, Hackenbush, I just don't know," he said with equal drama. "Oh, I know; we'll have the Thai guy bring some when he brings the food. Alan, quick the menu! The phone! But first," he looked around at them and let a beat go by. "Who's a vegetarian? No one? Excellent!"

Monty was slick enough to convince the Thai delivery guy to pick up some gin and bring it with the food. In an effort to conserve his energy, he sat back and let Hackenbush handle the conversation.

She zigzagged through a number of subjects but eventually wanted to know where Dr. Albany lived.

"Glendale."

"Upper or lower?"

"What?"

"Well, there's two very distinct Glendales," Hackenbush said rather brusquely. "Upper, especially the part around the Brand Library is very expensive, tidy and boring, and lower is very cool, affordable and has good restaurants. Where do you live?"

"Upper Glendale... but I only rent, so I could change very easily."

"House or apartment?"

"An apartment, but... I live alone, so my needs are few."

"In those miles of apartment buildings off Brand above Glenoaks?"

"Yes, but... well above Glenoaks, if that makes you feel better, Hackenbush."

"No pets, no plants, no lingering attachments?" she asked, pointedly not looking at Brazil.

"Afraid not," he said with his trademark hesitation. "But like I said... my needs are few and life is complex enough without pets, plants or, ah, lingering attachments."

"Possibly." She lit a cigarette and pinched a shred of tobacco off her tongue and glanced theatrically at Brazil. "Possibly you simply haven't met the right, ah, lingering attachment."

"So... what about you, Hackenbush?" Albany asked. "Pets, plants, attachments?"

"I have a broken heart, doc, I don't need anything else."

"That's the trouble with forming attachments; they usually end in tears," Alan said quietly.

"Some risks... are worth taking," Nathan said, also quietly.

"It depends on the risk," Alan said, even more quietly.

This was all so intense, they nearly jumped out of their skins when the Thai food guy, also bearing gin, rang the doorbell.

There was a brief wrangle about who got to pay for the food and booze that, much to Hackenbush and Monty's approval, Nathan won. Eventually the food and drink were doled out and they sat down to eat.

Around the middle of the meal Monty got bored with eating and, ignoring Alan's frown, lit a cigarette. "So, Alan, how is it I know about Inez's kid and Mrs. Azbury's budget items, but not about this perfectly charming man here on my right?" He waved pleasantly at Nathan. "Such secrecy is usually reserved for a clandestine love affair."

"Monty!" Brazil's blush undermined his scowl.

"And totally out of character for you, my dear," Monty continued. "However, what I've seen of Nathan this afternoon and Hackenbush's sterling recommendation, I can't think of a better match for you. I say you go upstairs right now and let us watch–"

"Monty! Um, no thanks," Brazil said when Hackenbush shoved another drink at him.

"Or at least listen at the door! Alan, you're a fool, as I have said many times in the past and–"

"So! Is there any more Pad Thai left?" Nathan asked, deftly cutting Monty off.

"No, Hackenbush ate all of it. As I was saying–"

"Aaand I wish you wouldn't, Monty." Nathan leaned toward his host. "You see... I... I occasionally have the misfortune of attending departmental meetings with Alan. These terrible meetings demoralize me, but... but they enrage Alan and he's beginning to show all the same signs here that he gets there."

"My dear Nathan, I'm merely trying to assist your cause," Monty said, laying one hand on his heart and the other on his guest's hand.

"My cause... well... that was probably lost the moment I walked in here," Nathan said calmly and looked at Alan. "So... I've invaded your home and privacy, drunk your liquor and generally behaved in the worst possible way. Alan, I apologize and I will leave... if someone wouldn't mind calling me a cab because I'm drunk as a skunk."

"Leave, Nathan? How can you think of leaving?" Monty asked. "This is one of the most pleasant evenings I've had in weeks! Alan, do something!"

"If you're feeling uncomfortable, Nathan, I–" Alan looked more uncomfortable than his guest, but nobody commented on it.

"Of course he's feeling uncomfortable! I'm throwing you at him, Alan!" Monty smacked the table with his palm. "Not that you're the most wonderful prize in the universe, but you're all I've got to throw at him right now. Possibly Hackenbush knows some nice young man we could introduce him to if you continue to be recalcitrant. Hackenbush?"

"Let me get back to you on that, Monty." Hackenbush leaned back and lit a cigarette.

"Please do, my dear," Monty said. "You see, I still believe Alan is perfect for Nathan, but, again, I've underestimated Alan's stubborn and persistent refusal to see what's good for him. After all, think of all the years he's wasted with me!"

"They've hardly been wasted, Monty, I–"

"Nonsense, darling, just imagine; with a little effort you might have found someone more amenable to condoms by now!"

"What?" Hackenbush asked in the ensuing silence.

"Nothing!" Alan snapped at her, so she just looked at Monty.

"Condoms, Hackenbush, condoms." Monty fixed her with so serious an eye that she could not help but listen. "You have before you a gay man who has endured the humiliation of sodomizing his lover wearing a condom."

"You mean before condoms became fashionable?" she asked, fascinated. "Really? Why?"

"Because Alan insisted and continued to insist until I simply lost interest in pursuing the project," Monty said coolly ignoring Alan's blush.

"But... that probably saved his life," Nathan murmured. Monty nodded but didn't look away from Hackenbush.

"But why did he insist?" she persisted. "Is there something I don't know about where babies come from?"

"I hope not, Hackenbush. Alan's issue was hygiene, not procreation; he is, after all, an M.D. and knows where babies come from, even if he has no truck with it personally."

"Hygiene?" she asked.

"Hygiene, Hackenbush. According to Alan, who is well-informed on such things, semen in the rectum causes the immune system to shut down in an effort to deal with a 'foreign' substance in the body. Or so he tells me."

"Really? Is it the same for women?"

"Oh, Hackenbush, for heaven's sake, you women are nature's sperm receptacles, aren't you? I mean the species would have come to a screaming halt eons ago if not."

"No, no, I mean up the ass," she looked earnestly into

Monty's bland face. "I mean, it's injury onto insult, since I think sodomizing women is just cruelty since women don't have a prostrate–"

"Prostate, Hackenbush, prostate," Monty corrected.

"Prostate gland to get off on," she said. "So, I mean, unless the chick is into it, the only one who's going to get off is the guy, right?"

"Isn't that always the case with you breeders? The guy gets off and then nine months later gets to change diapers," Monty said.

"Yeah, maybe," Hackenbush laughed. "But now there's a medical reason to say no to those weirdo guys. I can't wait to tell the girls."

"It's safe as long as he wears a condom," Alan said under his breath.

"Any idea how hard it is to get a guy to wear a condom for anything, doc?" She smiled at him. "You must be very persuasive if you got Mr. Swinger here to wear one for you."

"I was highly motivated, Hackenbush," Monty said. "By the way, Nathan, is it true?"

"That Alan is, ah, persuasive?" Nathan asked.

"Oh, we know that. No, is it true that semen in the–"

"Well... yes, it does impact the immune system," Nathan said carefully. "But usually by the time this is an issue, other, more imperative issues are in the forefront and hygiene is out the window. However, that does seem to be changing with the safe sex education going on these days. It is hoped that men are wearing condoms. We feel that anal sex is the main avenue of transmission for AIDS." He looked over at Brazil. "So... you've been in the vanguard, Alan."

"Hmmmm, and all this time I merely thought he was annoying," Monty said.

"Monty!"

"You are annoying, Alan; here I've found the one person in the known universe who could appreciate, even admire your fascination with rubbers and you–"

"Excuse me." Cold as ice, Brazil left the table. Somewhere in the house a door slammed.

"Think he'll be back?" Hackenbush asked.

Monty said no and suggested Hackenbush clear the table

and pour another round. "This will have to be my nightcap, friends, but you may certainly stay up."

"I really should get a cab home," Nathan said.

"All the way to upper Glendale? Don't be absurd," Monty said. "We have a perfectly good guest room. Oh wait, Alan lives in there. On the other hand, you could pretend you're looking for another room and once you're in there with him–"

"Ah, Monty," Nathan cut in, "I think Alan has had enough for one night."

"Possibly. Hackenbush, call the man a cab. How compassionate you are, Nathan," he continued while Hackenbush fumbled with the phone book. "You are going to have to force your way past Alan's defenses eventually. You must be strong, brave, resolute but also tender and clever, as Alan does not open himself easily."

"And don't forget the condoms," Hackenbush said, tipping the phone away from her mouth.

"Yes, well, thank you for your inviting me over. It's been extremely... interesting," Nathan said.

"I hope you'll come back tomorrow," Monty said. "The battle is hardly begun!"

"Hmmm... tomorrow, yes, well, it's nearly tomorrow now. I believe I'll, ah, get some air. Night."

Hackenbush watched from the window until the cab pulled away. She went back to the table, where she collapsed next to Monty.

"There's blankets and pillows in the hall closet," he said. "Be so kind as to wheel me into my bedroom before you pass out, Hackenbush."

She was, and then did.

Alan Brazil woke up with a slight hangover and an uneasy mind. First he cursed Hackenbush for introducing Nathan to Monty. It had to be Hackenbush; she was the only connection between Nathan and Monty. Then he cursed Nathan and Monty for being Hackenbush's dupes.

Then he thought about it a little longer and had to admit that the whole scene had been a Monty Vista production right up there with the very best Monty Vista productions. But he was completely convinced that Hackenbush was Monty's creature and that being the case, she would have to go.

He rolled over and tried to go back to sleep. In the process of trying to sleep, Alan found he was thinking how nice Nathan's gray eyes were. He'd thought that before, but thought they'd looked especially nice last night. And also what a nice speaking voice Nathan had. It was soothing and warm and low, nothing like the voice he used to talk over lab machines or ventilating hoods or Inez's radio. It was the kind of voice one could listen to all night.

All right, enough of that, it was time to get up anyway.

Downstairs he found Hackenbush asleep on the couch and got out his checkbook.

"You're fired, Hackenbush. Here's eight hours of pay, that I'm sure you didn't earn, and never come back here." He placed the check on her face and stepped back.

Hackenbush took the check off her nose and pulled the covers over her head.

"I'm not kidding, Hackenbush," Brazil warned.

"Kidding about what, darling?"

Brazil took a deep breath. "I've just fired Hackenbush."

"Really? I thought she worked for me, Alan," Monty said, slowly crossing the room and taking a seat at the table.

"How are you feeling, Monty?" Alan asked. Mornings were Monty's strongest time, but after all the drinking and smoking...

"Three hundred percent," Monty told him. "Never better! And do you know why, Alan?"

"Look, Monty–"

"Because I'm working again! And working with Hackenbush!"

"Monty, I–"

"And you want to toss out my muse like a used condom? Perish the thought, Alan! Not only would you be depriving the world of my memoirs, you'd be depriving Hackenbush of her greater destiny: to take her place among the greatest amanuensises or amanuensi, if you prefer, of all time; she'll be the Beckett to my Joyce; the Hobbes to my Bacon; the O'Grady to my Pound; the whatever to my whomever. How can you even consider depriving me, let alone the world, of my memoirs as recorded by the magnificent Dr. Hackenbush?" Monty ended his declamation with a resounding smack on the table.

"I..." Alan looked from his boyfriend to the bundle on the couch and then back. "I have to go to work now," and did so.

A muted applauding came from under the bundle on the couch.

"That was only round one, Hackenbush," Monty said when the singer peeked out at him. "This might be more difficult than I had hoped as Nathan appears to have less spine than I thought."

"Why? Because he didn't sling your boyfriend over his shoulder and carry him off to bed last night?" Hackenbush got up with difficulty and tottered over to the table. "Not everyone's a caveman like you, Monty," she said, lighting a cigarette.

"You look like shit, Hackenbush."

"You should see it from this side, dad. Feels like I have a layer of gin-soaked sandpaper under every inch of my skin." She pried a piece of tobacco off her parched lips and licked them. "But back to the Alan and Nathan situation; all is not lost, my dear purple-spotted one, all is not lost. I feel great hope and I feel we need reinforcements." She dug a hairbrush out of her purse and dragged it through her tangled locks.

"Reinforcements?"

"Yes, reinforcements. I also feel we need a Ramos Gin Fizz; just to cut the phlegm." She staggered into the kitchen disaster area and made a blender for them. "We'll think better after this," she said, clinking glasses with him.

"Reinforcements?" Monty prompted halfway through their drink.

"Yup; we need to have my band rehearse here," she said. "It will amuse you, annoy Alan and, God willing, drive him into Nathan's arms."

"You're a genius, Hackenbush, pure genius! Alan hates music!"

"What in God's name have you been doing with this guy all these years, Monty? He hates music, he likes condoms, he's uptight, he's—"

"He's just my Alan, Hackenbush. You've been in love; you tell me."

"All love did for me was make me stupid." She tilted her head and gave him a sidelong look. "Ah, well, maybe I do understand."

"Fuck you, sugar." Monty laughed at her.

"Pass on that one, brother."

"Now, really, Hacken–"

"Shhhh! I say that's Dr. Albany coming to fetch his car and that he will not come in and say 'good morning'."

"Or 'good morrow' as the case could be." Monty knew full well his hearing wasn't as sharp as the singer's, but cocked his head to listen anyway.

"Shit." She knew she'd heard him drive away, but went to the window to make sure. "Shit. Hmmmm, well, it's solvable; not to worry, Monty. I'll have him here tonight, by hook or by crook."

"I shall leave it in your very red and puffy hands, my dear," he said quietly and handed her a house key.

"Get some rest, Monty; you'll need it." She gathered up her things. "I'll be back mid-afternoon."

Hackenbush got home to her stuffy little apartment and cleared her machine. Not much interesting there; a call from Ross about the arrangements and a call from Shorty to see if she wanted to go have dinner at eleven last night. She changed her message to include Monty's telephone number if it was urgent or fascinating enough for the caller to leave a message and dial again. Dr. Brazil would probably hate that, but Dr. Brazil's life was really no longer his own now that Hackenbush had him in her sights.

She drank some water and was horrified to discover that it made her drunk all over again. There, proof positive that water is evil stuff and should be avoided at all costs. She switched to root beer, because it was quicker to open a can than make coffee, and felt better immediately.

To reclaim her morning and her morning routine, Hackenbush put some water on for coffee and took a long, hot shower. Usually a long, hot shower steamed most of the booze out of her but this gin substance seemed insidious.

Under the spray, she felt clean outside but pulpy inside, the way mangoes do when they've gone bad. Oh well, what coffee and vitamins B and C would not fix, a full agenda for the day would. She didn't have time for a hangover, however bizarre, so it would just have to subside to reasonable levels.

Amazingly, it did as she tided up her little space and began to plan her day. She had a moment of nausea when she stood up too fast, but a few puffs of dope from her glass pipe helped her over that. She rolled the remainder of her stash into joints, wrapped them in foil, and packed them under the tampons in her feminine hygiene case; something a girl should never be without.

Looking around her apartment, she'd be glad to be out of the scene of her most recent misery. Not to mention she'd be in a house with other people while the serial killer was still on the loose and would feel safer. And, in truth, she liked Monty and he seemed lonely like she was just then.

She called Shorty and left him a message to call her. Ross picked up the phone as she was leaving a message. "I found a place to rehearse, but it's kind of a weird deal," she said and proceeded to give him the lowdown on the Monty-Alan-Nathan situation.

"Hackenbush, how the hell do you get into these things?" Ross asked.

"Just lucky, I guess," she said, endorsing the back of Brazil's check. She'd run by the bank on her way back to Monty's place.

"I don't know about anyone else, but I'm not sure I want a guy with AIDS breathing on me."

"Don't you read the paper, Ross?" she asked, stuffing some clothes into a tote bag, just in case she was spending the night. "Gotta exchange bodily fluids with him to catch it. Or to be more blunt he'd have to fuck–"

"I get it, Hackenbush, I get it," Ross cut her off. "I also don't like the scheme to drive what's his name into what's his name's arms. That sounds like a bad, bad idea to me."

"Me, too, at first, and then I started to dig it," she said. "Look, Ross, just bring your drums and show up about three thirty today. We'll do one night there and if you hate it, we'll find somewhere else to rehearse. Have you found anything we can afford?"

"Not yet."

"Well, this is free so let's try it. You don't have to vamp anybody, you don't even have to be nice; just show. Could you please get Cody there, too? I'm running out of time to make phone calls."

"Mabel, Cody is not gonna like this any better than I do."

"Nonsense, daddy-o, Cody is much more of a romantic than you are. Bye." She hung up on his outraged snort, which was usually the best way to hang up on Ross.

She picked up the phone when she heard Shorty on the machine. She told him the when, the where, the why and to pack some clothes and bring a sleeping bag and that she'd pick him up at two. She grabbed her briefcase and ukulele case and was out the door.

"She wants us to what?" Cody asked and listened patiently while Ross ran it all down for him again. "Has she lost her mind?"

"No more than usual."

"I'm surprised, Ross, that you, such a sensible guy, would even consider this nutty scheme," Cody said, lighting a cigarette.

"Look, pal, I just want to rehearse and audition a new guitar player–"

"She's willing to consider that?"

"She will be when she realizes it's the only way I, and possibly you, will stick around these fags she's dug up," Ross said. "There's another thing: she sounds more normal than she's sounded in weeks. That's why I'm willing to try it."

"Normal?"

"Well, sober, conscious and sort of interested in life, which is what passes for normal in Hackenbush, I guess."

After a few beats of silence, Cody asked for the address and directions and said he'd be there at three thirty. Sharp.

"I hate grocery shopping, Mabel." Shorty said, following her swerving progress through the Echo Park Safeway.

"So do I."

"I hate it very much!"

"So do I!" She examined identical packages of pasta and tossed one in the cart. "That's why I like to do it in a team. Team grocery shopping; how else would I get through the dark twenty minutes of the toiletries aisle without being sucked into the hair care vortex? I mean, once I start reading shampoo bottles, it really is all over and I have to be forcibly removed. Besides, you've got something at stake here, Shorty; I'm going to soothe you all with a nutritious spaghetti dinner tonight."

"That's nice, Mabel, and no offense, but you're the worst cook I know."

"True, darlin', true; but I can reheat with the best of them." She waved a jar of spaghetti sauce at him.

He could not deny it, so they proceeded to the produce section where Mabel picked out some nice looking vegetables. She was rather good at making salads, so at least there would be one pleasant thing to eat at dinner.

Like Ross and Cody, Shorty didn't like the set-up Hackenbush described to him very much. The upside was that she was, or at least sounded and seemed, more alive and herself than she had been in weeks, which was all to the good. Shorty was sure life would go on without Hackenbush, after all even the best of friends have got to part someday, but he knew for fact it wouldn't be nearly as much fun.

Damn Eddy Lee for breaking up their happy little band in the first place. But oh, well, perhaps the best revenge for getting dumped was to get on with life with as much, if not more, flair than before.

They made a quick stop at an Armenian deli in lower Glendale for something called orange flower water and then drove over to Monty's place by South Pasadena.

"He might be sleeping," Hackenbush hushed Shorty on their way in. They tiptoed into the kitchen, shoved some dirty dishes aside and put the bags down. The good housewife that lives deep inside of everyone gave Hackenbush a momentary pang when she recalled, just barely, how immaculate the kitchen had been upon her arrival—children dear, was it only—yesterday. Oh well, if Brazil was a clean freak, and she suspected he was, this mess of a kitchen would drive him into

Albany's arms even faster. Heh heh heh. "Let me check on Monty and then I'll teach you to make a Ramos Gin Fizz."

Very quietly, she slipped into the dim bedroom and leaned over her employer. "Monty?"

Quick as lighting, he grabbed her, threw her on the bed and pinned her down. "Monty!" She considered yelling for Shorty but thought that would only make the wild look in Monty's eyes get even wilder. "Monty?" He seemed to be coming back from a long way off...

"Hackenbush?" He let her go and sat up. "Terribly sorry; rather thought you were someone else."

"I guess so, or you were planning to demonstrate some of your memoirs for me," she said, sitting up and straightening her clothes.

"Don't be obscene, Hackenbush."

"I'll try, Monty, I'll try. My dance partner, Shorty, is in the kitchen and on the verge of learning to make Gin Fizzes," she said. "Come out and join us. I gave him the lowdown on the Alan and Nathan scene and we can strategize."

"Excellent! And I've just the outfit to wear for it." He sent her upstairs to a storage cupboard for a garment bag.

Hackenbush had to drag it most of the way but eventually wrestled it into Monty's closet and left him to his sartorial transformation.

And was it ever worth it. Fresh from the shower and rosy, Monty strolled out in tuxedo pants, blinding white dress shirt, a magenta ascot and a deep amethyst smoking jacket that was so shiny, it glowed. Incredibly, or perhaps not so incredibly, his ensemble went perfectly with the purple spots.

Hackenbush and Shorty watched in something just short of awe as the fabulous old guy sauntered up to the table and eased his scrawny flanks into the wheelchair at its head. Hackenbush made the introduction and was amused by Monty's blasé acceptance of Shorty's handshake and curtsey. It was cute; they were both cute and Shorty knew a queen when he saw one and had the good manners to go with the insight.

"I believe I saw you dance once, Mr. Smith," Monty drawled, waving them to chairs. "Was it an evening you split with Donna McIntyre at some tiny tiny space on Vermont, say seven or eight years ago?"

Shorty was delighted someone remembered one of his obscure solo performances. "How nice of you to remember, Mr. Vista."

"Do call me Monty. I remember because you so reminded me of those wonderful photos of Nijinsky, before he went mad; perhaps a little after he went mad."

"Wow!"

When Hackenbush finished laughing and could speak again, she started to say, "What a rotten pick up line," but then she looked at Shorty. He looked positively enchanted so she simply said she didn't doubt Monty could seduce a Jain monk with a line like that.

"Only if he so reminded me of those wonderful photos of Nijinsky, before he went mad; perhaps a little after he went mad." Monty fitted one of Hackenbush's cigarettes into his holder and graciously let Shorty light it. "All right, Lieutenant Hackenbush; what's the battle plan?"

"We get the targets, Albany and Brazil, both here and drive them into each other," she said. "Simple." She snapped her fingers in a business like manner.

"Alan is easy; he lives here," Monty said, also snapping his fingers. "Nathan seemed unimpressed last night..."

"How could you tell? We were all drunk."

"Some of us were drunker than others, my dear. No, I thought he looked unimpressed and then when he didn't come in for a post mortem this morning, well, I was unimpressed. What about Shorty?"

"What about him?" Hackenbush asked, feeling nervous.

"For Alan."

"I'm too young to settle down," Shorty said helpfully. "Your Alan sounds swell, but he sounds better for this Nathan guy." He smiled innocently at Hackenbush's grateful look.

Monty shrugged and said, "Well, Hackenbush?"

"Okay, we get them here and then the band rehearsal starts," she said. "Maybe you can give us a few pointers, Monty."

"I'd probably have to be sedated not to, my dear, and I'd be delighted."

"Great. Oh, that's Cody or Ross, I hope," she said on

her way to the door.

It was Cody and his bass. Ever the gentleman, he laid it gently on its side and strolled over to be introduced to Monty. "Always a pleasure to meet anyone willing to give us rehearsal space," he said pleasantly and shook Monty's hand.

"Always a pleasure to meet someone who's not afraid to shake hands with me," Monty said seriously.

"If you could get AIDS from shaking hands, man, we'd all be dead by now."

"Ain't that the truth, pal. Wanna drink?" Hackenbush asked.

"A little early, isn't it, Mabel?" Cody asked, sitting down next to Shorty.

"Not for these." She waved at her vase-like glass. "These are nutritional type drinks." She rattled off the ingredients.

"Oh, well, that's different. And that's probably Ross; I was early, he's on time," Cody said on his way to the door.

Shorty and Cody helped the drummer unload while Hackenbush mixed up a blender of Gin Fizzes. They were finishing up when she came out with a tray of drinks, one for Ross, since she figured he'd want one. However, he seemed to be hovering on the far side of the room. Cody said something stern-looking to him and he finally sauntered over to the table. Hackenbush introduced him to Monty, but they did not shake hands. He did sit down next to Hackenbush and drink with them.

"This is good," he said after tasting his drink. "What is it?"

"Orange Julius with gin," Hackenbush said.

"You are commendably consistent, Hackenbush," Monty said out of the blue.

"Oh yeah?" Ross asked. As her drummer, he thought she was pretty inconsistent in her tempos now and then.

"How so, Monty?" Hackenbush asked politely.

"You have consistently handsome men in your band," Monty said. If he noticed Ross's fidget or Cody's smirk, he didn't mention it.

"Really? Do Ross and Cody remind you of Nijinsky, too?" She winked at the musicians.

"No, they remind me of an old, old ballet called *Arabian Nights* that some dancer named Aline something—I can't recall her last name—danced Scheherazade in. Quite wonderful; very much ahead of its time, simply chock-a-block full of beautiful black men. Ah, the good old days; now I only have the strength to look," Monty sighed, ignoring Ross's scowl as well as Cody's chuckle. "Well, how about if you all get to work?"

They drank up and moved to the instruments. Shorty stayed by Monty, who asked him where he would be in a performance.

"I'd be near the band."

"Then go there. A rehearsal should be as close to a performance as possible."

Shorty found a chair by the window. He didn't completely agree with that; he thought a rehearsal should be where you push the limits, try, fail, succeed and generally flail around like an idiot in the privacy of the bosom of your band. Occasionally *Dr. Hackenbush and her Orchestra's* performances were like that, but, as Schoenberg once said, "Sometimes an audience is necessary for acoustical purposes," and if they didn't like the show, they could go smoke and drink somewhere else. But he didn't contradict Monty Vista, who really was a famous director and choreographer, however retired and unjustly forgotten in this what-have-you-done-lately? town.

"What tune, Mabel?" Cody asked.

"'Let's Face The Music And Dance'." She inclined her head at Monty's tasteful applause for her choice.

Without a guitar or piano player, Hackenbush had to work a little harder and actually play real chords over Ross and Cody's tasteful four-bar into. Still strumming away, she took a breath and started to sing but no sound came out of her mouth. "Uhm, let's try it again, guys," she said with more poise that she felt.

Same thing.

Ross got up, stepped around his drums, and shook the daylights out of her.

"Okay, one more time," she panted, pushing her hair out of her eyes.

Ginger Mayerson

This time she made a sound, but a very puny sound, a very un-Hackenbush sound. The words were there if you strained to hear them; the rhythm, the melody were all there, but very quiet, like she was singing in a library and trying not to get caught. Even her posture was all closed up, her back hunched so her front was protectively curled around the uke, which she was holding so tight her knuckles were white.

Of course Hackenbush knew she was making a mess of the poor song. Her one hope was to get through this chorus, dance and get through the last sixteen bars. If Ross didn't kill her first. Poor Ross; he took her failures personally. He'd been angry when Eddy brought her into the band, but she really was a great singer, or had been, and he really was fond of her or had simply gotten used to her. At least that was Hackenbush's opinion. 'He'd probably rather see me dead than like this,' she thought, twisting the song out of her numb guts. 'I'd rather see me dead than like this.' But by then it was time to do something different. She set her uke in its stand and danced into the middle of the floor with Shorty.

This part was all right; she could rely on Shorty's choreography to make her look good. And it did; it made them both look good as they stomped around in a very limited space.

The stage for the October performance would be bigger, so Shorty yelled some directions and they glided around in bigger circles than clubs usually allowed them to. Hackenbush hoped she wouldn't get agoraphobia from all this space and distance. They danced two choruses and then she was back on the stand, with Cody and, more importantly, with Ross and his disappointments.

She finished the last sixteen of the song as badly as the first; worse, possibly, because she was out of breath and panting.

Everyone looked down at their instruments in horrified silence. Shorty looked at his feet; it was almost the same thing. The moments stretched taut, closing around the musicians and the dancer like a big fist about to pound them into oblivion. And then they were saved.

"Hackenbush, that was awful."

Four heads snapped up and glared at Monty Vista.

"Oh yeah?" Hackenbush snarled; looking, but not feeling, tough.

"Dreadful, pitiful, gruesome, hideous, terrible, appalling, and flat out bad," Monty said, puffing one of her cigarettes. "The dancing needs work, too."

"Hey!" Shorty sat up straighter.

"Darling, you're magnificent, but imitation Astaire is still imitation Astaire. Dig?"

There was more silence.

"Now come over here, children," he said, beckoning with an imperious wave. "I have things to say to the dancers and the rhythm section looks like it needs a drink."

"I'm with ya there, dad," Cody said, setting his bass on its side. "C'mon, Ross, you can kill her after the old guy gets done with her."

Ross put his sticks down and followed the band to the table. Hackenbush kept her ukulele with her.

"Gimlets for everyone, Hackenbush. Unless you gentlemen would like something else?" Monty was a wonderful host, really.

"What's Gimlets?" Ross asked.

"Gin and Rose's Lime Juice," Monty told him.

"Well, once you start with gin, you better stick with it," Ross said, glaring at Hackenbush. "What's this drink like, Mabel?"

"Rose's Lime Juice with gin," she said pouring for everyone. "It just is what it is."

Monty scowled at her. "Before I fix what's wrong with you, Hackenbush, call Nathan and make sure he'll be joining us tonight."

"Whaddya mean 'what's wrong with me'?" Hackenbush snapped.

Ross groaned from deep in his chest. It was a terrible sound. "Mabel, make that call for the man; he's got a lot to say to you. And then I have a few things to say to you."

"And I have a few things to say, too," Cody said quietly.

Shorty, next to the singer, simply reached over and patted her hand. She glared at him for his trouble. "Fine," she said and stomped over the phone by the couch. She did not bring it over to the table.

The men at the table sat in masculine silence listening to her inviting Nathan over for the evening. She was rebuffed, tried a different tack and was apparently rebuffed again. As a last ditch, she put Monty on, but he hardly got started.

"Delightful to meet you last night, Nathan, I feel we've hardly scratched the surface; you must come and dine tonight." Monty could be quite forceful.

So could Dr. Albany, who merely said he'd enjoyed the previous evening, thank you and good-bye.

"Damn." Monty chewed his lower lip and looked at Hackenbush as if it were all her fault.

"Plan B," she said. "Shorty, how about you go vamp Nathan and lure him here?"

"Lemme at him!" Shorty leapt to his feet.

"I hardly think Albany would go for Shorty," Monty said. "No offense, my dear, but Albany strikes me as, well, boring."

"Oh, you'd be surprised how charming Shorty can be," Hackenbush said, handing her dance partner her car keys and giving him directions to the lab. "Albany is tall, dark and handsome; clean shaven, broad shoulders and gray eyes."

"I thought they were blue," Monty said.

"It was the light reflecting off the gimlets that made them look blue; believe me, they're gray," she said.

"What's the other guy look like?" Shorty asked. "Just so I'm not confused."

"Tall, slender, brown-eyed blonde."

"I go for that," Cody said casually to Monty. "In women."

"Then Alan is safe from your Othello-like charms for the time being," Monty drawled.

Hackenbush clapped her dance partner on the shoulders. "Godspeed, Shorty."

Cody decided to go along for the ride. "Since you can't sing anymore, doc, I'd rather not stay here and fight about it. I'll let Ross stay here and fight about it. I'll see what's left of ya when I get back."

"Thanks, Cody, thanks a fucking lot," she snarled at his back. "It's not my fault!" she said to Monty and Ross.

"But it is your and the band's problem," Monty said

seriously. "Until they can you and hire someone else. And then you have a different problem, Hackenbush."

Hackenbush gasped and held her uke protectively in front of her.

Albany and Brazil could avoid each other for days at work. Usually they were just so busy in their own labs, their paths didn't cross much.

On this day, however, they were avoiding each other. Brazil managed to hold out until late in the afternoon before he came to Albany's lab. "About last night, Nathan..."

"I, ah, was out of line going to your home, Alan, I'm sorry." Albany leaned against his lab bench.

"Monty is a little flamboyant." Brazil rubbed his temples; his hangover hadn't given up yet. "I hope you weren't offended."

"Offended, Alan?" Albany asked, unconsciously gravitating closer to his, ah, colleague. "But... I thought he was wonderful."

"And he is wonderful and fabulous!" Shorty stalked into the room and planted himself in front of Albany. "How equally fabulous we have the same taste in men. Let's go have a drink and talk about it!"

The docs exchanged looks over Shorty's head.

"Um... I don't think we've met," Albany said making eye contact.

"I'm Shorty Smith." He shook hands politely and held on. "Hackenbush is right; you do have the most marvelous gray eyes," Shorty said, putting some smolder into it. "I don't usually go for gray eyes, but I could get used to yours, mister."

"Hackenbush sent you?" Brazil asked the back of his head and was ignored.

"Hackenbush sent you, Mr., ah, Smith, was it?" Albany asked, politely and politely disengaged his hand. "I'll be needing this later," he said, holding it up for Shorty to see.

"Oh, I do hope so!"

"In fact, ah, I'll be needing it now to show you the way out," Albany said, taking Shorty gently by the elbow.

"Why did Hackenbush send you, Mr. Smith?" Brazil

asked.

Albany paused in towing Shorty to the door and looked annoyed at Brazil.

"Because since you're not interested in this nice guy, she thought I ought to have a crack at him," Shorty said, in the most annoyingly matter-of-fact voice. "No sense a good-looking guy like this should be lonely because you're so... misguided."

Albany winked at the nonplussed Brazil. "That Hackenbush... always thinking of others," he said, guiding Shorty out of the lab. "Well, I hope that was that," he said when he got back. "He wanted me to come back to your place tonight; Hackenbush called earlier to ask me the same thing. Alan, I am so sorry that I intruded on your privacy, I..."

"It's Hackenbush. It's Hackenbush doing Monty's bidding." Brazil slumped against the lab bench and put his hand over his eyes. "You're an innocent victim in all of this, Nathan. I should be apologizing to you."

Brazil sounded so miserable that Albany stepped close enough to give his arm a comforting squeeze. "So... I understand," he said softly.

"Thank you." Brazil lowered his hand and looked warmly into Albany's eyes.

They jumped when Cody, standing in the doorway watching them, cleared his throat. "Which one of you boys is Alan?" he asked, roughing his mellow voice up as much as he could.

Albany moved protectively in front of Brazil, who stepped neatly around him.

"I am," he said, patting Albany's arm and crossing halfway to Cody. "And you are?"

"Cody Cole, doc," he said, moving slowly toward him. "How are you today?"

"Fine."

"Yesssss, I would say soooooo," Cody drawled, slowly circling the nervous white guy, looking him over. "Hackenbush sent me."

"Well, that was my next question," Albany said to no one in particular.

"The band is rehearsing at your place this evening,"

Cody continued, and continued to ignore Albany. He stayed focused on Brazil, as if this were the most fascinating creature he'd ever set eyes on. Personally, Cody couldn't figure out what the fuss was over this washed out guy, but there's no accounting for taste. And even he could see that these two guys were in love. Hopefully the other guy was Albany; he fit the description anyway. "And she wants you to pick up some gin and also some red wine that goes with spaghetti for dinner."

"I am not Hackenbush's maid," Brazil said, flushing a little with anger.

"I know, she's a bitch, isn't she?" Cody dripped with sympathy. "You can tell me all about it later tonight, in private, at your place. And you're beautiful when you're angry, man, did you know that?" he added, on his way out.

"Would you excuse me, Dr. Albany? I'd like to be alone," Brazil snarled between clenched teeth. "Oh wait, this is your lab. Please excuse me." Furious, he left the room with as much composure as he could manage.

Albany stood lost in thought for a few minutes and then called his sister and told her he wouldn't be able to make dinner that evening. If Shorty and Cody were part of Hackenbush's band, what on earth were the rest of them like? He'd find out because he couldn't see Alan facing them alone tonight. He called the number Hackenbush gave him yesterday (was it only yesterday?) and the line was busy.

"ee ain ee spthai fwsh maiwhee on ee phain."

"Very bad, Hackenbush; try again," Monty said. "And leave that spoon in your mouth."

"Hm, I'm not sure it's a diction problem," Ross growled.

"Perhaps not, but this is amusing."

"Well, that's true."

Hackenbush merely rolled her eyes over the spoon and began to try to declaim again. She was saved by the answering machine.

Like most people in LA, Monty screened his calls. Like a good secretary, Hackenbush rose to pick up when poor Alan began to demand that Monty pick up the phone. Monty waved Hackenbush back into her seat and the three of them listened to Alan become more flustered and angry, demanding to know what kind of people Monty was filling their home up with and ended with the line that he was "not going to pick up gin and red wine on his way home!" and slammed down the phone.

"Why do we need red wine, Mabel?" Ross asked.

"I'm making spaghetti for dinner; Shorty must have told him."

"I thought Shorty was going to seduce Nathan back here," Monty said. "Although I rather doubted the success of that; it was like sending Jerry Lewis to seduce Clark Gable."

"Who knows what happened?" she said. "All I know is we've got to find a liquor store that delivers."

"Why bother, Mabel? That angry man on the phone is going to toss you out on your ass when he gets here," Ross said reasonably.

The phone machine clicked on and Monty told her to get it when Nathan's voice came on the line. "Nathan, how delightful! So wonderful you can make it tonight," Monty drawled. "Hackenbush is making spaghetti; how about picking some red wine and more gin? No? Well, then we see you tonight." He hung up. "Charming man, still perfect for Alan if only Alan would see the light. Bring the directory over here, my dear, I think there's a liquor store around here that delivers. Yes, and do take that spoon out of your mouth and wash it, there's a good lass. And make us another round while you're at it."

Cody and Shorty showed up just in time to tell their stories over drinks.

"Well, you shook something loose," Hackenbush said when they were done. "Both targets will be here tonight, hopefully moving toward each other."

"They were definitely leaning toward each other today," Cody said. "How's her singing, Ross?"

"Probably the same, but her diction is better."

Hackenbush merely scowled at them while Shorty opened the door for the liquor laden delivery guy. Monty set up an account since it looked like they were going to be there for the duration.

Monty was retelling some pornographic incident, accompanied by Hackenbush on the uke, when Alan stormed in and demanded they all leave.

"Alan, darling, welcome home," Monty drawled while Hackenbush continued to comp. "This is Ross, I believe you've met everyone else. Fix yourself a drink, I'm in the middle of a story."

Brazil stomped out of the room and then a door slammed upstairs.

"And this is our other host, Mabel?" Ross asked with a sneer.

"Exactly!" she said.

"Now where was I?" Monty said and launched back into his story. At the end of it he suggested, well, told, the band to play so he could at least see what the dancing needed.

Having nothing better to do, the band and Shorty ambled back to the far end of the room. Cody wanted to see what the dancers were doing for or to "Them There Eyes".

Somewhere in the middle of it, the doorbell rang and, not missing a beat, Shorty danced over and answered it.

Stepping into a dance and band rehearsal is always disconcerting, but Nathan did a pretty good job of regaining his poise. He edged around the dancers and set the bag in his arm on the table by Monty.

"Nathan! Welcome!" Monty pushed the bags out of his sightline and kept watching the dance in progress.

"I'm sorry if I was, ah, brusque on the phone earlier," he said sincerely. "I brought the wine and gin."

"That's wonderfully kind of you, dear man; we can always use more gin. No such thing as too much gin," he added, frowning at Hackenbush's sloppy pirouette. "Take your coat off; stay a while."

"I..."

"MONTY, ARE YOU WATCHING THIS!" Hackenbush screamed, stomping her foot.

"Oh shit," Ross said, putting his sticks down.

Cody leaned over his bass and said, "Well, we ain't seen this show in, what? Six, seven months, Ross. Looks like a good 'un coming on."

"You like looking at car wrecks, too, Cody," Ross murmured under Hackenbush's screams.

"It's an acquired taste, old man," Cody chuckled; at least

he was enjoying the show.

"AND WHAT THE FUCK ARE YOU TWO DOING?" Hackenbush swung round on her band.

Shorty had wisely retreated a safe distance from the tantrum. He vaguely wondered how long it would last without Eddy here to shake her out of it. Ross might try, but he'd probably just get punched in the jaw for his trouble and that would be worse.

Under the cover of all this, Alan had come down and put an affectionate hand on Monty's shoulder. He greeted Nathan cordially and looked at the scene in progress.

"Ah, the good old days," Monty sighed while Hackenbush caught her breath. "Screaming, shrieking divas everywhere." Monty placed an equally affectionate hand on the hand on his shoulder. "Magnificent, isn't she?"

"Well, that could be a word for it," Alan drawled, smiled wryly at Nathan and went into the kitchen.

Hackenbush had not resumed her tirade after Alan appeared and went into the kitchen; she remained silent, waiting.

Not for long. Alan poked his head out of the kitchen and, stony faced, beckoned her in. She picked up her ukulele and squared her shoulders. "If I don't come out in five minutes call an ambulance," she said bravely.

"Oh, Hackenbush, I'll handle this," Cody said. He smiled wolfishly at Nathan as he strolled past him and into the kitchen.

Alan immediately came out and sat between Monty and Nathan. "May I have a gimlet?" he asked.

"Hackenbush, if you would be so kind," Monty said.

"Shorty, you handle it, please," she said, putting her uke down. "I guess it was time to start dinner anyway." She went into the kitchen and found Cody in there, convulsed with laughter. "If you're done terrorizing Dr. Brazil with your smoldering charms, wanna help me cook dinner?" she asked, trying not to laugh and filling a big pot with water. "God, if he only knew what big pussycats you and Ross are."

"Then he'd really feel stupid," Cody finished for her and put the pot on the stove.

"Yeah, yeah, yeah. Let's go drink and be sociable while

that boils."

Being sociable mainly consisted of listening to Monty talk about his life in the theater for a while. He was capable of carrying a conversation for miles, but he tired easily these days and soon ran out of steam.

"What do you all do in your lab?" Shorty asked Alan and Nathan in the lull.

"Medical research," Nathan said.

"Like, with animals?" Shorty asked.

"Sometimes."

"You're docs; know much about AIDS?" Ross asked blandly.

"A little," Nathan said.

"We actually know quite a bit about AIDS. Don't we darling?" Monty said, patting Alan's hand.

"It's not a very pleasant subject," Alan murmured.

"It's a mystery, ain't it? Nobody knows nothing," Hackenbush growled. "Do they?"

"I hear it's incurable and I know it kills you pretty quick," Ross added quietly.

Nathan sighed. He hated these kinds of conversations and avoided them like, well, the plague. But Alan looked so uncomfortable and Monty was watching him carefully. Perhaps this was another stupid test to prove what a great guy he was. Part of him wanted to say the hell with all of this, let me live my lonely empty life in peace, but a bigger part wanted to prove what a great guy he was. "So... that seems to be what we're seeing in the lit... in the cases recorded so far," he said, nodding at Ross. "It's transmitted via blood and semen; possibly, although less likely, by tears and saliva, but it would take a gallon of either to get enough virus to take hold in a healthy system. Doctors think there will be a therapy in about fifteen years..."

"We'll all be dead by then," Cody said.

"I heard that doctors say 'fifteen years' for anything they don't have a clue about," Ross said neutrally.

"Well, it means that doctors have identified how and why the virus kills the host," Nathan said equally neutrally. "But... in medical history, it usually takes about fifteen years of research to find a therapy to stop or slow down the virus' course. Sometimes it takes longer."

"Well, as long as there's a cure in the works, I guess there is something to look forward to," Shorty said, trying to brighten things up.

"Not a cure... a therapy to slow it down," Nathan corrected, but gently. "Right now people die within three to seven years after being diagnosed. Depending on their overall health, a therapy might give them another ten to fifteen years of life."

"That's all?" Shorty asked, stunned.

"That's a lot of life to get through, if you think about it, Shorty," Hackenbush said bitterly.

"But no cure?" Cody asked.

"No... no cure, and as far as a cure, or even a vaccine, goes, right now we truly don't have clue," Nathan said, hoping the discussion was winding down.

"So condoms and clean needles for all!" Shorty said. "They ought to hand them out on street corners."

"Neva happen, baby," Monty said.

"Not with the puritans we got running the gov these days," Ross said coolly. "Worse than that, some people think the gov put this in the population to get rid of the people they don't like."

"Yeah, I heard that, too." Hackenbush perked up. "Like an experiment in biological warfare or something."

"To kill off the queer and needle loving populations of our enemies?" Monty asked. "I'm sure the Evil Empire is shaking in its boots as we speak."

"Like us!" Hackenbush clinked her glass with him.

"Well... I've heard this rumor, too," Nathan said reasonably. "Our government has done some odd things but this kind of assault..." he trailed off looking at Ross and Cody.

"There were some black men in Alabama that died of syphilis so our government could study how syphilis kills a man," Ross said quietly, looking at Nathan.

Nathan met his gaze but said nothing. He knew about the Tuskegee "study" and it made him sick.

"Yeah, no one told them they had it, were dying of it." Cody picked up Ross' thread. "And being men, as men will be, they spread it around, so the suffering just gets multiplied and went on and on and on."

"Your tax dollars at work!" Hackenbush drawled coldly. "See how efficient our government can be when it puts all its amaaaaazin' resources into a problem." She shrugged. "Problem for who, well, that's another story."

"Problem, what problem?" Monty asked. "As long as it's only the queers and junkies dying... since when is that a problem? Let's use those tax dollars to buy more china place settings or sail those obsolete battleships around the seas in a display of obsolete, but touchingly nostalgic, Amurrican Naval might."

"Hey, if you love a man in uniform," she said and rolled her eyes in perfect unison with Monty.

Nathan cleared his throat. He couldn't defend what happened in Tuskegee, but thought he should stick up for science (if he could). "So... I don't have, ah, all the details but that study was the work of a very small number of researchers–"

"For forty years?" Cody asked.

"Proof positive that government work will kill you if you let it." Hackenbush seemed not so much to be talking as attitudinizing with words. She must have realized she was being an ass and took herself into the kitchen.

"You all seem very well informed," Nathan said calmly. "And... very bitter."

"We've all lost someone to AIDS, doc, we know how ugly it is," Shorty said quietly.

Ross nodded. "We also wonder why we never hear about it on the news much. Most of what we hear is from AIDS Project LA or word of mouth. Sometimes the paper, but not too much."

"The Times? Their Hollywood coverage is spectacular and the only reason to ever open the damn thing," Monty said. He got frowned at and was puzzled by that.

"I think the reason there's so little press on AIDS is that so far the affected population isn't that big," Alan said, trying to take some heat off Nathan.

"Not yet; but almost everybody has sex, doc, don't they?" Cody said coolly. "I mean, I've heard of monogamy, but never knew anybody that did it." He looked up at

Hackenbush, leaning on the door jamb, listening. "What about you, Mabel? Ever hear of monogamy?"

"Yeah, it was something I was working on with Eddy Lee, the bastard," she said, lighting a joint. "Now I'm just knocking myself out. Grad-u-lee by de-grees."

"That looks good, Mabel," Shorty said with a hopeful look on his face.

"Here," she dug a fresh joint out of her purse and handed it to him. He shared it with Ross and Cody; the docs declined.

Hackenbush stood next to Monty and offered him what she was smoking.

"I'm afraid I'll get cooties, Mabel," he said.

"You're not afraid of anything, Monty. Neither am I."

They passed it back and forth until there was nothing left of it. "Thank you, Mabel. That was quite nice," he said.

"Yes; ours had a little hashish in it." She turned to go back into the kitchen. "For medicinal purposes only."

"And dinner is when?" Ross called after her.

"Sooner than later. 'Scuse me," Cody said and followed Hackenbush into the kitchen.

Possibly the dope had mellowed Monty to the point that he could reminisce with ease. On the other hand, Monty could always talk about himself with ease. He had an audience happy to listen to things that happened before they were born. This went on through the mediocre spaghetti dinner Hackenbush eventually put on the table. Thank God Cody decided to make garlic bread; it was the best part of the meal.

"You'd better learn to cook if you're going to catch a new man, Hackenbush," Monty said, lighting a cigarette. He either ignored or didn't notice Ross', Cody's and Shorty's horrified looks.

"I'm through with love, Monty, but if I did want to catch another man, I'd probably use nets and curare-tipped darts," she said, picking up her uke and strumming a few chords.

"Well, he'd be a quiet one that way," Monty agreed.

This seemed to be a conversational dead-end.

"I've been thinking about your name, Monty," Cody said after a few beats of silence went by. "Isn't Monte Vista a street up in Highland Park?"

"Yes, that's why I picked it," Monty said serenely. "I

thought it was more memorable, more Californian than Myron Cohen."

"Myron Cohen," Hackenbush echoed, strumming her ukulele.

"Yes, maidela, yes," he sighed.

In the awkward silence that followed, Ross, who was heavily bored, picked up a cigarette package wrapper, ripped it in two and began to accompany Hackenbush's rambling chords. He watched her carefully; she was relaxed and playing and even breathing in her old familiar way, something he hadn't seen in a long time.

Cody and Shorty were watching, too. Without singing a word, Hackenbush was weaving a spell, not unlike the one she used to, in the old days. Hardly knowing what he was doing, Cody gravitated to his bass and began playing along with the uke and cellophane percussion.

Hackenbush breathed down into herself and fixed Alan with one of those killer diva looks, and glory hallelujah, began to sing "Let's Call a Heart a Heart" very nearly like her old self.

Alan fidgeted. Hackenbush thought he looked cute doing that. She hardly noticed Ross moving to his drums she was so intent on the doctor.

"I think I'll clean up the kitchen," Alan said, rising under Hackenbush's intense gaze.

"Nonsense, darling, leave it," Monty said, patting his hand, wondering what Hackenbush's point might be. Would be interesting, whatever it was.

Alan got up anyway. Nathan volunteered to help but was politely rebuffed. When he turned back, he found Hackenbush, still playing along with the band now, standing in his path.

Over the years of navigating bars, Hackenbush had become adept at herding people. She herded them with her voice, with her body and gentle taps of her uke. She was now maneuvering Alan this way and that, and doing a fine rendition of "Let's Call a Heart a Heart" while she was at it.

With one final menacing stomp she tipped Alan into Nathan's surprised lap. She tossed her uke to Monty, who was roaring with laugher and shouting "Brava", and danced off with an elated Shorty.

She had danced and danced competently, but now there was joy in her dancing. And when she sang the last sixteen bars she simply lit up the room.

Alan had eased off Nathan's lap with an awkward apology and then stayed to watch Hackenbush cavort with Shorty. "She really is good," he whispered to Monty under the applause.

"Never a doubt, darling, never a doubt," Monty drawled, handing the uke to Shorty for its return to Hackenbush.

The band spent the rest of the evening getting to know each other again. Hackenbush was in especially good form, but tired easily. She was also playing her uke hard to make up for the lack of guitar player. "We gotta get somebody but quick, cats," she said between songs.

"That was always the plan, Mabel, we just never knew if you were coming back," Ross said with a tired smile.

"Oh, well, now you'll never get rid of me," she answered vaguely.

"Maybe we can do auditions here tomorrow?" Cody suggested, watching Alan and Nathan talking softly.

"Yeah, sounds good," Hackenbush murmured; she was also engrossed in watching the 'targets' moving closer. "Ah, progress; if I accomplish nothing else here..." she thought, but said, "Let's do 'A Fine Romance'."

They did and quite nicely.

Eventually, Monty told them to call it a night. Nathan looked at his watch and decided he should go home but promised to come back tomorrow when asked, or rather when ordered, by Monty.

"Same time tomorrow?" Ross asked.

"Can it be a little earlier? I'm giggin' tomorrow night," Cody said over his shoulder.

They established a time when they could all be there. Ross said he'd put the word out for a guitar player.

"You can give the guitarist this number, if you like, Ross," Monty said.

"Much obliged, Monty, much obliged." Ross wrote the number in his book and left with Cody.

Hackenbush and Shorty gave the kitchen a quick once

over. "Thank God they have a dishwasher," Shorty said, taking the blender apart and putting the pieces in the machine.

"Yes; how civilized." Hackenbush wiped all the flat, visible surfaces.

She gave Shorty her car keys so he could get home. He then told her that his boyfriend's wife was back and he, Shorty, had nowhere to stay. "Man, Shorty; how many ways has it got to be true that you ain't had no trouble 'til you mess with another woman's man?" she asked, handing him her apartment key.

"Only until you don't get a kick out of saying it, Mabel; then something else will be true." He kissed her cheek and told her he'd see her tomorrow.

She poked her head into Monty's bedroom to say good night to him, but he was sound asleep and smiling rather wickedly, too. She realized how exhausted she was and fell into her bed on the couch. "Is it singing or living that's wearing me out?" she wondered, but fell asleep before she got an answer.

Dr. Brazil left for work early the next morning and stayed late holed up in his lab the next evening to avoid Hackenbush. He'd overheard the rehearsal plans and that Cody (who was not unattractive, but just a little scary) would be leaving before nine for a musical engagement. So, he worked late, hoping that the band would be gone by the time he got home.

He was also hoping Monty would give up his nutty scheme to pair him off with Dr. Albany. It had failed with Monty's old theater friends; it would fail with Nathan. As touching as his lover's concern for him was, Brazil really felt that there couldn't possibly be anyone after Monty. Monty Vista was enough lover for one, if not more lifetimes.

And he was happy with Monty, who didn't make any demands on him emotionally or physically. Those days were long gone. They'd grown closer since Monty became ill, but although he felt great tenderness for him, Alan was beyond passion. Life was simpler like that and he planned to keep it that way.

He'd loved Monty passionately once; it had been uncomfortable and eventually became excruciating. He was happy this way; tepid, as Monty called it and Monty was always right, of course.

This mess with Hackenbush would all die down fairly soon. After all, didn't the girl have a living to make somehow and somewhere else?

"I see you're still here, too."

Brazil glanced up at Dr. Albany standing in the doorway. "I thought I would finish a few things up," he said, gesturing to his nearly empty desk. "And I'd like to avoid the carnival at my place for one night."

"I was wondering if that was the case; I've gotten two calls tonight asking where we were," Albany said, coming into the room.

"From whom?"

"One from Hackenbush and one from Shorty."

"Ah, Shorty; your admirer." Brazil smiled. "What do you think of him? He seems to like you a lot."

"I think... he'd bore me very quickly," Albany said seriously. "I think we have nothing in common and I'm too old to try to make a life in someone else's world."

"Like I tried with Monty," Brazil thought, but said, "Show business people are flamboyant, but usually very nice."

"Yes... quite nice; notice the trouble Hackenbush is taking over Monty."

"I think Hackenbush has a streak of cruelty," Brazil said, letting his anger show a little. "She's playing with Monty, leading him on and letting him think she can help him." He looked up at Albany, who'd said nothing, and found the doc watching him with interest. He felt a flush rise in his cheeks and grabbed up some papers on his desk. "I don't mean to keep you, Nathan, I'm sure you have other things to do."

"It's dinnertime... let's go have dinner."

"I have a lot to do here."

"I can bring something back for us."

"No, thank you, I won't be here much longer." Brazil looked at his watch.

"Well, then... I'll see you later," Albany said, turning to go. "I promised I'd look in at your place on my way home, just for a quick one."

"Hackenbush has too much influence with you," Brazil

murmured.

"Possibly... she tells me I amuse Monty, and that's the most important thing, isn't it, Alan?   Amusing Monty." Albany waved and was gone.

Brazil watched him go and then looked at the clock. If he waited another thirty minutes, he would definitely miss Cody at home and possibly the rest of them. On the other hand, if he'd gone out to dine with Nathan, he'd have missed them all just the same and he would have had a nice dinner. As it was, he ended up having some lukewarm old coffee with lots of Cremora in it and calling that dinner.

"More chow mein, Nathan?"

"Thank you, no, Monty. I suppose I should be going." He glanced at his watch and looked around at the crowd in the room.   Upon his arrival he was introduced to three guitar players and four saxophone players, all of whose names he'd forgotten already. According to Monty, who was enjoying the jam session immensely, the guitarists were there to audition and had decided to stick around since Hackenbush was in such good form again.   Evidently the word was out and the sax players were there for the same reason; Hackenbush was a dream now that she was singing again.

But, although he could admire the beauty of her voice and found the way she sang the words attractive, Nathan thought there was something cold and forbidding about her. If he let his imagination run away with him, Nathan could almost see her using the song as a shield between her and, well, everything but the music and the moment.   She was pleasantly laid back between songs and listening very attentively when others were playing and a vision when dancing, but when she was singing there was the oddest hostility in it.

And then into the middle of it all, Alan came home, looking exhausted and annoyed. Hackenbush tilted her chin at him but he was otherwise ignored.

"Want some chow mein, Alan?" Monty asked when his lover got within shouting range.

"Thanks, no, darling," Alan managed to say between his clenched teeth. "How long do you suppose all this," he waved at the band, "will be going on?"

"Hard to say; I think they haven't reached the arc of their trajectory yet." Monty looked up sympathetically at Alan and patted his hand. "Poor Alan. You missed Cody," Monty said, a trifle too innocently. "But your luck seems to be changing." He nodded at the door, where a tuxedo-clad Cody had just come back in carrying his bass.

Cody tilted his chin in the Alan-Monty-Nathan triangle's direction and then waved at the band's shouts of "Cody! Cody!" He unzipped his bass case and took up his usual place on Ross' left.

And the song went on and on. Alan excused himself and went upstairs to put his briefcase down and change clothes. He heard the song change to something slower and sadder and then turn into something brighter and certainly faster. The shouts and laughter and stomping led him to believe Hackenbush and Shorty were dancing, but he had no way to be sure.

Eventually that song ended and there was musical quiet, but lots of moving around and deep voices. The smell of cigarette smoke and a sweeter smell drifted up to his bedroom. He recognized this smell and thought he ought to go down and throw them all out, but didn't quite have the courage for it. A little later the front door opened and closed a few times and he heard cars start and drive away. He thought it might now be safe to go downstairs in his own home.

He was mostly right; only Dr. Hackenbush and her Orchestra and Nathan were sitting around the table with Monty. "Join us, darling!" Monty called him over.

"Yeah, sugar, where you been?" Cody asked, patting his knee.

As sexy as Cody was in tux, Dr. Brazil seemed to find the invitation to sit on his knee highly resistible.

"Here, Dr. Brazil, you can have my chair," Shorty volunteered and then perched on Dr. Albany's knee.

Alan ignored all this and simply got a chair from the kitchen. When he came back, he found Shorty on Monty's knees and wondered vaguely what Nathan might have said to Shorty to cause that. Or possibly Monty said something to cause it, anything seemed possible in his house lately.

"Cody was just telling us the police closed the club he was supposed to perform in tonight," Monty said, easing Shorty off his lap and back into a chair.

"Oh," Alan said politely.

"No idea why," Monty continued. "Seems a shame to waste such an attractive man in a tux."

"I hate this outfit more than I can tell you, Monty," Cody said, tugging his cuffs down for the nth time that night.

"No doubt; all sensible men do," Monty agreed. "The remarkable thing is how a tuxedo tips a man so far into ridiculous that he becomes magnificent. It's either an indication of how far we've come as a civilization or just the opposite."

"I don't think fashion, male or female, is much of a measure of progress, Monty," Nathan said with a chuckle.

"Neither do I," Hackenbush said, tucking her cigarette under the D string just beneath the tuning peg.

"What do you use, Hackenbush, music?" Nathan asked.

"Dentistry."

Ross winced but stayed quiet.

"Dentistry?" Alan asked, curiosity momentarily overwhelming his desire for these people to leave his house.

"Yeah, dentistry. Whenever I feel nostalgic for some past I've never lived in or despair of the modern world, I just think about the history of dentistry," she drawled. "And then I don't feel so bad."

"When the drill bites, when the needle stings," Shorty sang. "When I'm feeling pain!"

Monty roared and the band laughed politely because they'd heard it all before. The pair of docs exchanged amused, but dry looks.

"Mabel, how many ukuleles are you going to burn up in one career?" Ross asked, pointing to the tuning pegs of her instrument.

"Fuck!" She yanked the smoke off the neck, burning her finger in the process. At least Ross had noticed before any damage was done. She had in the past let her unfiltered cigarettes burn into the wood and snap the strings due to inattention and occasionally due to strong drink. "Thanks, dad," she murmured, putting some ice on her finger.

"Oh, by the way, Alan; Shorty will be sleeping on the couch in your office tonight," Monty said.

"Don't these two have homes?" Alan asked, glaring at the dancer couple.

"Yes and no, but the point is they're staying here," Monty said, closing the subject.

"Unless Dr. Albany wants me to stay at his place," Shorty said hopefully.

"Um... if I had to choose one of you... I'd rather take Hackenbush home with me," Nathan said and then blushed.

"Upper Glendale? I hardly think so," Hackenbush said tiredly. "And frankly, I don't sleep well outside the city limits."

"I believe I'll say goodnight," Cody said, looking softly at Alan. "Unless I get invited to sleep somewheres."

"Say goodnight, Cody," Ross growled under Monty's laughter. "I gotta go, too. Mabel, which one of those guitar players did you like today?"

"None."

"Same here; try again tomorrow," he said and towed Cody over to pack up. They were gone very quickly.

Alan handed a pillow and blanket to Shorty and went to bed himself.

Hackenbush walked Albany to his car. "You're a good sport, Nathan," she said, lighting a cigarette. "I think you're making progress with him."

"I'm a fool, Hackenbush," he said looking at her in the streetlamp light. "I don't see how whatever your fiendish plan is to get us together is going to work, but... I've pinned all my hopes on it. Like I said, I'm a fool."

"Cheer up, doc; he's weakening, I can tell," Hackenbush said.

"I'm not sure I want someone you have to wear down for me to get," he said.

"Oh, pooh! I don't know him well enough to know exactly what the resistance is, but I can see it waning or something." She tossed her smoke into the gutter. "Monty says he's just lazy because they've been together for so long. But let's face it, they aren't going to be together that much longer and Brazil is going to need someone to lean on, whether he wants to admit it now or not."

Albany stared at her for a full minute while he digested this speech. "What a... ghoul you are, Hackenbush," he said, opening his car door.

"I'm a realist. If that makes me a ghoul, well, these are ghoulish times we live in," she said. "Nothing I can do about that, doc, but roll with the punches."

Since he had no answer for that, Albany merely waved and drove off. She stood on the curb until he was out of sight and then continued to stand there, enjoying the quiet and the cooling down nighttime city.

Then she slumped a little and thought about Eddy Lee. He'd said in that last phone message that he loved her but wasn't ready to settle down. The gutless bastard could have made the effort and told her in person. Now she had long hot days to think it over and over and over and soon she'd have a winter to face without him. '"Love will make you happy/ask anyone that you know/chill you to the marrow/if your love runs cold", as they say,' she thought. She had a small pang of jealousy of Monty; he'd be out of this mess sooner than later and had had a whale of a time in his life. 'But I suppose those days are gone for everyone,' she thought. 'Hell, I'm only twenty-eight and feel older than God's wet nurse. Oh well.'

She was about to turn and go in when she heard a low engine purring toward her. A dun colored sedan came along with no lights, paused before Monty's house and turned on the brightest lights Hackenbush had ever seen before it went on its way and around the corner.

Hackenbush shivered; it was too cool and too quiet out there so she went into the house.

"Mabel, do you like any of these guys?" Ross was fuming over his tuna casserole. He'd gotten sick of take out and Mabel's terrible cooking and taken matters into his own hands. Tuna casserole and salad; even Monty (who no longer noticed much about food) was enchanted with dinner. "Well? How many guitar players do I have to drag in here for you to frown over?"

"How many more ya got?" she asked innocently. She saw Cody suppress a smile but knew he was as annoyed with her as Ross.

"None. Pick one or we start looking for a piano player," Ross growled.

"Oh, no, not that! Not a well tempered instrument!" As good as she thought her intonation was, Hackenbush still liked to work with instruments that had a little play in their tone. She looked to Monty for help, but he looked like he was a million miles away. "All right, guys, any of these three will do: John Brill, Al Juarez or Philip Noyes. Pick out the one you like best and I'll learn to live with him."

"You sure, Hackenbush?" Cody asked.

"As sure as I can be," she said. "I like the way these guys play; pick one and if all of us can work with him, well, that's great."

They settled on asking Phil Noyes just as Alan got home.

"There's more food in the kitchen, Alan," Ross said over his shoulder as he was dialing up Noyes with the news.

"Thanks." Alan was tired and hungry; it was nice to come home to food that looked good for a change. He got a plate and sat across from Hackenbush. He was next to Cody, but he'd discovered that Cody was unthreatening when Nathan wasn't around. "This is good, Hackenbush."

"Ross made it; he's a better cook than I am and almost as good as Cody," she said. "Where's Nathan tonight?"

"I've no idea; I'm not in charge of Dr. Albany," Brazil said slowly. "Where's Shorty?"

"Picking up some gin; we're out again," Monty said.

Brazil looked at him carefully; Monty seemed exhausted. "Are you all right, Monty?" he asked.

"Yes, but I need gin, Nathan and Shorty to fully revive me," Monty said, lighting a cigarette. "Ah, and here they are; right on cue." He waved at the dancer and the doctor.

"Did you run into each other at the liquor store?" Hackenbush asked.

"Yes." Nathan handed her a fifth. "Um... could I have my drinks with vodka, please? The gin is taking its toll."

"Your wish is my command, doc." Hackenbush started mixing gimlets while Shorty and Nathan got food for themselves. "I hope gimlets go with tuna casserole," she said.

"They go with everything, my dear, simply everything," Monty said, downing half his drink. "But back to business; where were we?"

"What did Mr. Noyes have to say?" Cody asked Ross.

"His machine said he said leave a message at the tone and he'll call us right back." Ross started picking up empty plates.

"How adorably coy." Hackenbush got up to help Ross but he waved her away. "Sounds like something I'd say on my machine."

"Well, it's not a 'no', is it? I liked that Noyes guy," Shorty said.

"Us, too, Shorty," Cody murmured, looking hard at Alan.

"When will you start the real rehearsals?" Monty asked. "The ones with the horn section?"

"Next week. God willing and the creek don't rise," Ross said. "And if Mabel finishes copying the parts."

Hackenbush wiggled her ink stained fingers at him. "I'm copying as fast as I can, Ross; you wanna break out a pen or pay for another copyist, I'm all for it."

"Yes, dear," Ross said. He picked up the plates and went into the kitchen.

"Well, back to work, you lot," Monty said, perking up.

"Can I smoke a cigarette, dad?" Hackenbush plunked herself into a chair and lit up. "And wait for Ross? I hate trying to work without a drummer."

"Yes, dear." Monty mimicked Ross perfectly.

"You don't seem to get out much, do you, Alan?" Cody asked in the ensuing silence.

Everybody stared at Cody, and then at Alan.

"I go to work quite a bit," Alan said politely.

"When was the last time you went to the movies?"

"I can't remember." Alan looked at Monty, who shrugged.

"Well, I have a movie for you and Dr. Albany there to go see," Cody said, whipping a copy of the LA Reader open. "It's called *Buckaroo Banzai*, and it says here: 'Adventurer rock musician Buckaroo Banzai and his band, the Hong Kong Cavaliers, take on evil alien invaders from the 8th dimension.'"

"That sounds like something I could stay home and see, Cody," Alan said, sipping his gimlet. He rolled his eyes at Nathan.

"All right; how about *Brother From Another Planet*?"

"Hmmmm."

"Okay, what about *Dreamscape*? This guy can visit people in their dreams; saves the president and gets this blonde babe."

"Pass."

"*Love Streams*, directed by John Cassavetes, starring–"

"Oh, we liiiiike him," Monty interrupted.

Alan smiled patiently and said, "You know, I think I'd just like to have a quiet evening at home with Mon–"

"You know," Hackenbush cut him off. "That's a great idea, Dr. Brazil. I've been meaning to ask you again about this thing you have for condoms anyway."

Everybody looked at Alan.

"Condoms?" Shorty asked when the silence had gone on long enough for him.

"Okay, Nathan, let's go!" Alan leapt to his feet.

"Wha...? Which film?" Nathan asked pushing his chair back.

"We'll figure it out in the car." Alan snatched up the Reader and was out the door with Nathan in his wake before anybody could say condoms again.

The band and Monty had the good manners to wait until they were sure they were gone before they laughed like hyenas. "Bravo, Cody, bravo!" Monty cheered.

Everybody applauded.

"What brought that on, daddy-o?" Hackenbush asked.

"We've been selfish, Hackenbush," Cody said. "We've been so caught up in our own stuff, we lost sight of the fact that we're, or you're, trying to throw those two together. I thought, now that we've narrowed it down to three guitar players, we should get back to work on getting them together."

"Well, I'm glad somebody's thinking these things," Monty said. "Even I'd lost sight of the original mission. Well done, Cody, and thank you. Now, back to work. I hope to see better dancing tonight than I did this afternoon."

Phil Noyes called back and said he'd be delighted to be their guitar player. He had a free evening so he joined them and the rehearsal went very well indeed.

"Hackenbush, I want you and your musicians out of my house," Alan said, trying to talk over the blender the next morning. He'd been horrified to find Cody, who was breaking up with his girlfriend, had moved in and was sleeping on a cot near Hackenbush's couch. "This is my home and not some kind of commune." He might have said more but Shorty handed Hackenbush the blender and he and Cody took themselves and their breakfasts into the backyard.

"Really, Dr. Brazil," Hackenbush drawled over the rim of the blender. "I'm not sure what you're more distressed about: that Cody is staying here; that he has or had a girlfriend or that he's sleeping on the cot and not, ah, somewheres else. If you know what I mean."

Brazil flushed dangerously, but Hackenbush stood her ground. She could almost feel sorry for the guy. Almost; she'd probably never really feel sorry for any man ever again. "Oh, by the way, here's my bill for the week," she handed him a neatly typed invoice.

"You're charging me for invading my home?" Brazil asked as he read the bill. "What's cartage?"

"The cost of Ross and Cody dragging their stuff in here," she said. "Tho' Cody won't need it until he finds a new place to live and that could take a while."

"'Supplies?'" he asked, quoting from the invoice.

"That's broken down into liquor, food, cigarettes and miscellaneous."

"What constitutes 'miscellaneous'?" he asked.

"Contrabass and ukulele strings, India ink, pens, part paper."

"'Mileage'?"

"How do you think we've been getting to and from the liquor store, dad?"

"I thought you might be riding your broom, babe," Brazil snarled and shoved the invoice at her. "I'm not paying this. I fired you on Monday, but you didn't go away. I'm not paying for you to annoy me or manipulate or exploit Monty or–"

"Manipulate or exploit Monty?! Who has me dancing my feet into stubs? Who's ordering me around like a... a..."

"A what?"

"A secretary!" She put the blender on the counter and squared off with him. "And you know, Alan, we're doing this all for you, you selfish bastard. You want your house back, fine! Start shacking up with Dr. Albany here, everybody's happy and we'll all leave. Except Monty, he lives here. And he now lives to see you be happy and you're just being an assho–"

"Excuse me." Shorty stepped briskly into the kitchen. "Since the windows are open, everyone can hear you; including Monty, who would like to see you for a moment, Dr. Brazil."

Brazil took a giant step away from Hackenbush and left the room.

"He was about to smack you, Mabel," Shorty said quietly.

"So what?" She poured more gin in the blender and let it whirl around. "I'm only sorry Monty heard that," she said.

"His bedroom overlooks the patio," Shorty said, helping himself to some fizz. "Cody and I were kind of enjoying it, until we saw Monty standing at his window."

"Was he annoyed or distressed?" Hackenbush wondered why it mattered to her.

"Couldn't tell; the guy is kind of inscrutable sometimes," Shorty said. "Anyway, we were distressed all the sudden and he asked me to send Alan into him. You should have some food with your gin, Mabel," he added as she downed the last of the blender.

"Why?"

"Because Ross will kick your ass if you're too drunk to work today," Cody said, standing in the doorway and looking annoyed. "And so will I." He gathered up some dishes and started to wash them.

"Tough love, Shorty, it's a beautiful thang," she snarled and started to make herself some eggs. "Could you hear what's going on in Monty's bedroom?"

"No; they're keeping their voices down," Cody told her. "Don't push your luck too hard with Brazil, Hackenbush, he looks like he's got a temper."

"Luck... luck is for rabbits," she said vaguely. "Can't be much of a temper, Cody, or he'd have killed Monty by now."

"I think it's a selective temper, baby, and that you should be careful."

"Yes, sir."

They heard the front door slam and since they didn't hear anything else, they figured Dr. Brazil was on his way to work. "Shorty, go see if Monty wants a drink, okay?" Hackenbush asked.

Shorty came back quickly and said Monty wanted a Ramos Gin Fizz. He also wanted Hackenbush and her invoice.

Hackenbush stuffed some scrambled eggs in her face while Cody made the drink. She took it to Monty, who was nicely propped up in bed.

He patted the mattress next to him. "My dear Hackenbush, sit here and show me your invoice," he drawled and complimented her on the drink.

She told him Cody made it. He said nothing as he perused the invoice. There was a rather uncomfortable (for Hackenbush) silence.

"Hmmmm, well, my dear, if you rewrite this so it's just for your time," Monty said at last, "I'll pay it. I'll try to wedge some money out of Alan for your expenses, but he's very tight; where do you think all this came from?" He waved at the room in a general way.

"I'd rather get it from Alan," she said.

"Never happen, darling, and besides, what money I have is actually Alan's money. What difference does it make how you get it? As long as you get it."

"Oh, well, in that case, okay."

"I knew you'd see reason," Monty said. "And since I have you here, all to myself for a change, let's have a little chat, shall we? I had a long talk with Cody the other day while you were running errands. He said you nearly drank yourself to death over this man who got away. Really, Hackenbush; no man is worth it when you can always find another one that's just as bad and death is so very final, my dear. Don't you want to know how it all turns out?"

"Maybe it's not worth the trouble, Monty," she said quietly. "When Eddy loved me it was all so much easier to cope with the bullshit. All I've ever wanted to do was sing and have a good time. Then I fell in love, got dumped and now nothing is good enough."

"How spoiled you are, my dear."

"No, not that, not really," she said. "It's bigger than that. When Eddy left me, I woke up to what an empty, pointless life I have. I don't fit into mainstream, normal America; never could and never have. I just visit it in temp jobs when I need money and God knows I avoid that as much as possible. Let's face it, Monty, I haven't got much of a future; no one especially gives a damn about people like me. Not even me."

"Then you're a little fool, Hackenbush, if you think that has ever mattered to making art," Monty told her. "No one does care what you do or how you do it until they see it; until something inside of them goes very still while listening or watching and this mundane, everyday trivial reality we all live in falls away for a few moments. Ah, those moments. This might have slipped your mind, dear, but those moments are worth every drop of blood we sweat for them. Those moments are, in fact, all the pay off there is for us. And most people never will see that because it's rather frightening; it's so much bigger than anything they're used to. But that you see it, that you live in the moment when you can; when the lights go up and you look out into the void and call it home. And in that moment, you might, just possibly might, reflect a little of the cosmos back here for those poor bastards sitting at the bar. That's all you can do, my dear, that's all any of us can do. So fuck your future; you probably don't have one and wouldn't like it anyway if you did."

"Very mystical, Monty, but I didn't understand a word of it," she said after a moment of trying to figure it out.

"Of course you do; you've just got it confused with death, when it's only surrender," he said. "Someday you'll discover that the difference between wanting to die and dying is vast vast vast."

She mulled that over.

"And as far as anybody caring about you, well, I can name three men right off the bat that care very much," he said. "But let's face it, kid, I can tell you with a fair amount of certainty that the dominant social group and the Reagan administration do not care about you."

"Why should they? I hate and disagree with them," she said.

"Good point, but you have no power and they do," he said seriously. "Dangerous stuff, power; one false move and it becomes despotism, cruelty and horror."

"Well, Monty, I think Reagan's a prick, but last time I checked we were still a democracy," she said.

"All the parts we can see of it, yes; but how little we know, my dear, how little we know."

"Hmmmm."

Monty patted her hand. "Yes, hmmmm. And so much for your education for today," he said. "I need a nap; wake me this afternoon, just before Alan gets home. And please call Nathan; I'm so enjoying having him here in the evenings. Makes me feel young again!"

Hackenbush closed the door softly behind her and went into the front room. Ross was there with a backpack, sleeping bag and air mattress. She looked at him and then his stuff and then him again.

"Don't even ask, Mabel," he said coldly.

"Well, if you're going to be around here, you can help me copy parts," she said and offered him a Gin Fizz.

Hackenbush came back from running errands, one of which was to go to the bank to deposit Monty's check before anyone named Alan could put a stop on it. Shorty met her at the door and took the shopping bags from her.

"Big Daddy Hackenbush called," he said.

"Oh yeah? What's he want?"

"He wants you to call him." Shorty wandered off into the kitchen with the groceries.

Hackenbush sat down next to Ross and Cody, who were copying parts, and lit a cigarette. Monster musicians and fine cooks they might be, but she only considered them fair, bordering on good, music copyists. Their parts were legible and since she was glad for the help, she could hardly complain about their lack of obsessive detail in the parts. Not everyone was as obsessive as Hackenbush (who required each of her noteheads to be the exact same size throughout each part) and that probably just made it that much of a saner world.

"You gonna call your dad?" Cody asked.

"Dunno. How'd he sound?" she asked, pinching a piece of tobacco off her tongue.

Cody shrugged; he'd never met Louis Hackenbush, he didn't know what he was missing.

"Neurotic as ever, Mabel," Ross said. He had met her father on a gig once, before he met Mabel, and was unimpressed. "Call him; find out what he wants."

She sighed and dialed. "Hi, daddy, this is Mabel, returning your call, you can call me back at... oh, you're there... yeah... no, you didn't hear wrong; yeah, Eddy Lee dumped me... No, I've no idea why it took him so long..."

"Hang up!" Ross hissed.

She winked at him but didn't hang up. "What? Aunt Marie said what? ...that he's an idiot? Well, maybe, but what does she really mean? That he's an idiot to dump me or that it took him so long to do so? Well, ask her next time you see her; I'm simply dying to know now... Yes, Ross and Cody are still around... Shorty too, and we hired a new guitar player so you can stop worrying... Oh, you weren't worrying, well, that's good... Yes, me too, daddy, I hope everything will be fine, too... You what? Oh, yeah, the La Mirada Lanes... No, I've never had the pleasure of gigging there..."

"A bowling alley?" Cody asked.

She nodded and rolled her eyes. "Yes, daddy, I'm listening... You want what? You want Ross and Cody tomorrow night?" She looked up at Ross and Cody, who were now listening with interest. "Well, I don't own them; work it out with them. Here." She shoved the phone at Ross, who was closest to her.

Hackenbush sat smoking and pouting and trying to ignore Ross' conversation. It was just typical of her father to steal her bass and drummer when she was down and out. He didn't even ask her to come hear him play. He knew she wouldn't go, but she still liked to be asked. She looked up when she heard Ross ask if there was a dance floor.

"Good, then we're bringing your daughter and Shorty," Ross said. "And you need a guitar player, too? I'll see what I can do." He hung up.

"Oh ho! Now I'm singing in a bowling alley!" Hackenbush snarled.

"When was the last time you sang anywhere in public?" Ross asked her. He was dialing so he didn't pay much attention to what she said next. "What?" he asked, pulling the phone away from his ear.

"I said, why did you accept this gig, Ross? You hate my father; my father hates black people; I hate it that my father hates black people; I–"

"Phil! Can you gig tomorrow night? Call me ba– Oh, you're there... Shit, you can't... s'okay, I know a guy in Orange County... Yeah, Moody! You know him? Oh... Well... Y'know, I just close my eyes and listen... Yeah... Next week... rehearsals, see ya." Ross hung up and looked at Cody.

"Moody?"

"Yeah; Moody," Ross said, digging his book out of his backpack. "He's amazing."

"And a great musician, too," Cody said, smirking.

"As I was saying about my father–" she began.

"Mabel, your father is not unusual," Ross cut her off. "Like many assholes, he hates everyone except the people he knows and can't stand most of them either. But fifty bucks to play standards in a bowling alley is still fifty bucks." He picked up the phone and started dialing. This indicated to Hackenbush that he'd lost interest in their conversation.

She flopped into a chair next to Cody. He reached over and patted her shoulder. "Honey, don't worry, we all got problems with some member of our family," he said. "I'm looking forward to meeting your old man."

"No, you're not."

"Now, now."

"Cody, one time he was going on and on about how Black people on welfare were ruining this country and I got fed up and called him a racist," she said. "You know what he said?" Cody shook his head. "He said: 'Mabel, honey, I'm

not a racist; I just don't like niggers on the beach.'" She lit a
cigarette and blew out an annoyed plume of smoke. "I didn't
speak to the bastard for six months; he didn't even notice."

Cody looked horrified. "Um... Ross?" he began when he
could speak.

"Hold on, Moody," Ross said and took his mouth away
from the phone. "Cody, Louie Hackenbush is a jerk, a fucking
jerk, excuse me, Mabel, but he's a pretty good woodwind
player, neurotic, like they all are, so just ignore him. And
ignore Hackenbush; she's all gloom and doom and doesn't
understand her old man any better than I do."

"Or like him better," she snapped.

"Yes, you do."

"No, I don't."

"You're his daughter," Ross said.

"So?"

"Mabel, cool it; you're scaring Moody," Ross said and
went back to his telephone conversation.

Hackenbush shrugged and smiled wryly at Shorty,
coming out of the kitchen. "We're dancing in a bowling alley
tomorrow night, pal," she said with a sneer.

"On the lanes or in the bar?" he asked. "Well, it's a gig,
is it not?" he asked when she just stared across the table at
him.

"I'm not sure our luck is changing, but it's certainly just
got more interesting," Ross said, winking at Cody. "Moody
can make the gig."

"No doubt, since no one can stand to look at him and he
never leaves his house," Cody said.

"Moody is a huge guitar player. So huge, he's
sometimes called Moby," Ross said, smiling evilly.

"Yeah, Moody the great white guitar player," Cody said,
smiling equally evilly. "Five foot five and three hundred
pounds of burning guitar playing love."

"Oh, excellent," Hackenbush sighed. "If this guy is so
great, why isn't he working tomorrow night?"

"Well, like Cody said, he hates to leave his house and
drive anywhere, so he only does gigs in a certain, very
restricted, part of Orange County. That is, if you catch him in
a good mood and ask him nicely," Ross said. "We're lucky

that La Mirada is in his driving range."

"He'll like you, Mabel, he likes brunettes," Cody drawled. "They go so well with his white hair and blue eyes."

"Oh, how nice for me."

"He'll get along with your dad," Cody continued. "Moody hates everyone, too. Especially the people he knows." He went back to work copying the bass parts for the show.

"He likes music and is an incredible guitarist," Ross said, picking up his ink pen again. "That's all that matters to me."

Mabel nodded and picked up her pen. She wiped the nib, pulled some part paper in front of her and began to copy a tenor saxophone part for "The Song Is You".

The three worked in silence until Shorty brought out some coffee and sandwiches for them.

Neurotic as ever, Louis called back to find out if Ross had, in fact, gotten him a guitar player.

"You handle this one, Ross," Mabel said, rolling her shoulders.

Ross picked up the phone and brought it over to the table. "Yeah... Yeah... What horn section? You have a horn section on this gig? You do? It's a bowling alley... No, never been there... Okay okay, I believe you, it's a nice bowling alley... Hold on." Ross put his hand over the mouthpiece and looked hard at Hackenbush. "Your old man's a nutcase, Mabel," he said. "He's got two brass and two woodwinds on this gig and he expects us to just show up and jam."

"I never said he wasn't a nutcase," Hackenbush hissed back at him. "See if he's got charts on the songs," she added, relenting a little. "That might be helpful."

Ross went back to his conversation and a few seconds later Cody and Hackenbush were horrified to hear him giving Louis directions to chez Monty.

"Are you nuts, Ross?" Hackenbush snapped when the phone was firmly on the hook.

"He's just going to drop off copies for us to look at," Ross said blandly.

"No, he's not; not my old man," Hackenbush shot back.

"He's going to show at about dinnertime, so we'll feed him. Then he's going to want to go on and on about his wonderful arranger, who is not me since he thinks I have no talent. Then he's going to whip out his clarinet and force us to play music with him. And worst, worst of all, is if he talks to us about his philosophy of life. We'll be lucky if we can get him to leave before three am."

"And who might that be, Mabel?" Monty asked. He strolled across the floor and sat in his wheelchair at the head of the table.

"My father."

"Your father is coming here? How delightful!" Monty helped himself to some coffee. "We'll have to do something special for dinner."

"Like put thorazine in his food," Cody said quietly.

"Does he like that?" Monty asked.

"Like it or need it, is a better question," Hackenbush said darkly.

"Probably both, Monty," Cody said. "I hear he's a terror."

"Never met him?" Monty asked. "Well, a treat for both of us."

"I've never met Big Daddy Hackenbush either," Shorty put in.

"I wish you wouldn't call him that, Shorty," Hackenbush said. "Makes him sound, I dunno, cuddly or something."

"Hm, I would say cuddly does not describe him," Ross said. "Look, Monty, I'm sorry I invited him to your house without asking you first. We'll try to get rid of him quick as we can."

"Tosh, Ross! My house is your house!" Monty flashed a huge smile around the table. "And I love meeting new people. I've met so few in the past few years, your stay here has been completely delightful for me. Invite all the hipsters and weirdoes you want!"

"Yeah, well; thanks, I think," Ross said. "I personally have never had any problems with Louis; it's Mabel who gets tense with him."

Mabel shrugged and went back to work copying parts.

If anybody noticed Hackenbush watching the street around dinnertime, they kept their mouths shut. She was edgy; the threat of seeing her father always did that to her. Deep down she loved him; it was on the surface that he annoyed her.

Their differences were mainly political. He'd voted Democrat in every election while he raised her and then voted for Reagan, which Mabel found inexcusable, after she moved out on her own. He'd become a jerk in a lot of ways; partly it was age and disappointment, partly it was ideology. The age and disappointment touched Mabel's core; the ideology enraged her. He was also a womanizing jerk, but that was none of his daughter's business. From him, she'd learned that men are strange creatures and to expect the unexpected. To her detriment, she'd forgotten it with Eddy Lee.

But she only had one father in her life and he was a doozy. He was kind of a cutie; even Mabel knew that. He had a wiry build and was a little taller than his daughter. He had a nice full head of nut-brown hair and beady brown eyes to go with it. Mabel's hair and eyes were darker, like her long gone mom's, and she'd inherited her mother's sturdier frame. This was why, she was sure, she could hold her liquor better than her father, who squiffed out pretty quickly when he drank (which was why he seldom drank).

So she loved him and avoided him so she could keep on loving him. He was one of the multitude of angry white guys that emerged in the last election. Guys, and gals (she supposed there were some), who thought everyone else was getting a better deal. As if supporting a kid in Los Angeles on $550 per month, food stamps and MediCal was a better deal. As if living in a box down on San Pedro and Fifth was a better deal. As if waitressing for minimum wage and what tips you might get was a better deal. What planet did these angry people live on? And why the hell were they so intent on grinding the poor and working poor under their heel? On her good and generous days, she thought it might be because the angry types were afraid of the people they wanted to punish and afraid they might become like them. Well, it was always possible. On her bad and cynical days, she thought it was because the angry types knew that the poor and working poor were pretty much at everyone's mercy and could be tortured with impunity. They were voiceless and helpless and an easy target for rage. The lesson she garnered from all this thinking was never owe anyone anything; it was bad for their personality. They might start to think they had some power.

Therefore the country elected Ronald Reagan, a guy who said and acted like poverty and despair were lifestyle choices. And people who knew nothing about poverty and despair ate that up with a spoon. Then Reagan told us that the poor were not shouldering their share of the burden of keeping our country great so they had no right to complain about how it was run. But please notice, there's now employee taxes on unemployment benefits (as if that makes any sense at all), and notice the extra eight percent tax on waitress' wages, usually minimum wages, supposedly to cover all those tips the waitress might or might not get (and who hasn't stiffed a waitress at least once?), and notice that income tax (which people with no income do not pay) goes down but sales tax (which everyone pays) goes up; so who's shouldering what in our great country now?

It all made her sick. She didn't really care if the rich got richer, but shouldn't we all be getting richer? Reagan's rising tide for all boats seemed to have gone out, but everyone Hackenbush knew, including her father, were still standing on the dock, which was collapsing under them.

But her father was still a Reagan fan, he felt the country needed a strong hand in these troubled times. She'd once foolishly asked, "What troubled times?"

"Well," he said. "Inflation is out of control."

"So, by cutting taxes so people have more money to spend on yachts is going to slow it down? Don't taxes have to go up so people will stop spending? Or would it just be better if we all lost our jobs and didn't have any money to spend?" she asked.

"You know nothing about economics," he'd said.

"Yeah, well, neither does your Ronnie boy, daddy-o," she'd snarled. "Anybody who thinks if you build more nightclubs, more people will go out and spend money in them, while at the same time trying to get inflation down by making it impossible for anyone, except his rich pals, to get or spend any money, is asking for trouble. It's like bailing your boat with a spaghetti strainer; might look good but is ultimately futile." She hung up on him before she really lost her temper.

Dr. Hackenbush might not know anything about economics, but she did know when she was getting fucked and not even kissed.

She'd liked Carter; he seemed like a decent guy, one who really did care about everyone. But he lost and America is a county that cannot abide losers, however endearing they are. We are a great country, or so we are told. God forbid anyone, like President Carter, might suggest there might be room for improvement.

Frank Sinatra was another problem. Her father adored Sinatra; upbeat Sinatra, downbeat Sinatra and God help us, he loved that maudlin album Frank made of Rod McKuen songs. It was one the major truces of their relationship when Mabel allowed that Sinatra was acceptable when paired with Count Basie and Louis had agreed not to play any Sinatra without the Basie band around her. Had they not come to this agreement, they might have killed each other by now.

They seldom worked together. Mainly it was geography: Mabel covered LA and her dad got Orange County. He disliked LA very much, so it was probably a major concession for him to drive all the way up there to talk about the gig. Of course, he'd stolen her bass player and drummer, and then Ross had gotten him a guitar player, so there might have been an element of gratitude in his coming up to see them all, the jerk.

She was in a foul mood; not even Monty tried to jolly her out of it. Alan came home to find a very subdued group around the table, asked no questions and gave them a wide berth. Nathan was working late and would not be joining them. Well, that was all right; Mabel herself would rather not be joining them, but she was stuck.

As predicted, dinner was almost on the table when Louis showed up.

"I don't know how you people live up here in the traffic. Hi, doc honey." He gave her a buss on the cheek (she was grateful he took the cigarette out of his mouth before he did) and shook hands with the band. "What's with that guy's face?" he asked in a whisper after he met Monty.

"Acne," Mabel whispered back, disinclined to deal with her father's paranoia and his other weird prejudice against gays.

"Like I was saying, I don't know how you people live in this traffic," Louis said, dumping a stack of charts on the table.

"More like we live around it," Ross said distractedly as he glanced through an arrangement. "Louie, these charts are for a big band."

"We can use the format," Hackenbush said over his shoulder as she pushed the packs of paper around. "Oh..."

"What's wrong, my dear?" Monty asked.

"Nothing." She shoved a chart on top of what she was looking at.

Cody dug it out and said, "Oh..."

"'Oh...' what, for God's sake!" Monty snapped. He hated people being mysterious around him.

"Oh... 'Body and Soul'," Ross told him. "We can do it without you, Mabel," he said to her.

"Why should we?" Louis asked. "I like the way doc does it."

"Thanks. It's just... well, I have new insight into it, that's all," she said quietly.

"What? Eddy Lee? Darlin' you gotta get over that someday," Louis said and shrugged. "I mean, if you let a man bring you down you ain't gonna get far in this life, honey."

"I must remember to write that in my diary," Hackenbush murmured. "Y'all want dinner first or music and then dinner?" she asked.

Ross smiled and said, "Dinner first." Hackenbush father and daughter had a mild southern drawl that neither of them seemed to be aware of. They were speaking a little more slowly and their "A's" were a little broader and mellower than he recalled they were ten minutes ago. Maybe they were just relaxing around each other, but he doubted that; Hackenbush was (amazingly) more tense than before.

As they were sitting down, Nathan called and asked if he could join them. Without consulting anyone, Alan went to the phone and said of course.

"I'm impressed you got Moody to play guitar, Ross,"

Louis said, while Hackenbush was dishing up lasagna for everyone. "Did you drop my name?"

"Save some for Nathan, please, Mabel," Alan whispered to her, and she said she would.

Ross shook his head. "No, didn't mention you, Louis," he said. "Moody and I go way back, before he gained weight and became a recluse."

"That's funny because he called me for directions to the Lanes and a song list," Louis said. "Just wondering, because he doesn't like me."

"How do you know?" Cody asked.

"He said, 'I don't like you Hackenbush, but I'm playing on your gig tomorrow.' And then he hung up on me," Louis said.

"Maybe he called the Lanes and found out who he was gigging with," Ross speculated. "Moody's about the smartest guy I know; no reason for him not to find out who he's working with."

"But if he doesn't like you, why is he playing the gig?" Shorty asked.

"Moody hates everyone, Shorty, but he likes Ross if he thinks about it," Cody said. "Unless he's just being masochistic."

"No, he's doing me a favor," Ross said. "But Moody really loves to play once he gets to a gig. We're just lucky it was the right time, the right place and he was in the right mood when I called."

"Why is he a recluse?" Hackenbush asked.

"Usual reason: a woman," Ross told her.

"Since when is that the 'usual reason'?" she snarled.

"Always. He got dumped and decided it was safer to stay home," Ross said matter-of-fact like. "Now he leaves the house sometimes and if he runs across a woman... He just looks and then ignores her."

"Sounds like sound advice," Cody said with a wry smile.

"What about men?" Monty asked suddenly.

"I think he's straight, but doesn't care about men any more than he cares about women," Ross said. "Although I do think he feels more comfortable around men because he's never been dumped by one. I can relate to that."

"Me, too," Cody said.

"Yeah," Louis agreed.

"I can relate to the opposite of that," Hackenbush added. "Shorty?"

"I'm too young and innocent for this conversation," he said, batting his eyes. "Monty?"

Monty smiled inscrutably and Alan didn't comment at all; he was too busy letting Nathan in and getting him some food and drink.

"How do you know these docs, doc?" Louis asked after he was introduced to Nathan.

"I worked a temp job for them," she said.

"Well, I'm glad you're keeping a roof over your head," Louis said. "These are tough times for your average Joe."

"Who said I was average or Joe, daddy?" she asked but knew he was not listening.

"At least we've got a president that knows what he's doing," Louis said.

"Since when? And it's not November yet, pal," she shot back. "If we're lucky, we might not have him for much longer."

"Oh, please. You really think tits and Fritz have a chance in hell?"

"I'm praying as hard as I can."

"It will take a miracle," Louis said. "At least the economy is turning around."

"For who?" she asked and waved off Monty's grammar correction.

"For everyone."

"How so? I'm working temp jobs for the same money and my rent still goes up once a year," she said. "Unless you're living off your tax cut, dad, you're in the same boat as me and it's sinking fast."

"It's going to take some time, doc. We got a lot of freeloaders in this society; leftovers from the Sixties," Louis said, lighting a cigarette. "The nig– the people on welfare aren't going to disappear overnight."

Hackenbush flushed dangerously and ground her teeth. "You're good at blaming people who can't defend themselves, dad," she snarled.

"Hey, I work and get a check; they don't work and still get a check," he said. "It's about the same amount of check, too. So, baby, who needs defending here?"

"You can work; they can't–"

"More like won't."

"So, take their check away and let 'em starve?"

"They can get jobs."

"You looked in the want ads this year, dad? Not much out there," she said, calming down a little. "And in LA if you have to ride the bus to work, that costs money and is a nightmare. And if you have kids, forget it. I temped with a woman paying three hundred a month for childcare and that was the cheapest she could find. And then food and rent and–"

"Nothing can't be overcome with initiative," Louis said.

"Completely right, Mr. Hackenbush!" Monty said suddenly. He smacked the table and continued. "Huge deficits, bloated military, corrupt officials, unpaid-for evening gowns, a tax cut that's only useful for about five percent of the country, and deregulation everywhere you look. I expect the economy to come surging off its knees like a stallion after a mare in no time. There'll be chicken for dinner every night and jobs, maybe two jobs, for everyone!"

"See, Mabel, this guy's got the right idea," Louis said.

"Monty!" Hackenbush was floored. She assumed Monty was a great actor but this was very convincing. The band and the docs looked shocked.

"Flay the course! Isn't that what the Reagan campaign is saying this year?" Monty asked.

"Exactly!" Louis looked pleased. "And 'It's Morning in America', too."

"Yes! Exactly!" Monty turned to Mabel and bellowed: "It's morning in America, Hackenbush, and you're working the night shift!"

Hackenbush compressed her lips not to laugh and couldn't look at her father. She suspected from his silence that he was puzzling over that last remark and, though she had issues with him and his politics, she wasn't black hearted enough to laugh in his face.

Ross cleared his throat and suggested they play some

Ginger Mayerson

music. Hackenbush excused herself to go into the kitchen,
ostensibly to warm up her voice but also to laugh like a hyena
(but quietly, into a towel).

As foretold, Louis had brought his clarinet and they
settled down to run through the arrangements. All went well
until they got to "Body and Soul". Ross, Cody, and Shorty
seemed resigned to what was about to happen but the rest of
the room was completely unprepared for the heartbreaking
intensity of Hackenbush's singing.

"Body and Soul" was an easy song to get wrong and
very few singers got it right. In fact, there were very few right
renditions of it in existence. Hackenbush had struggled with it
for quite a while and collected versions of it. She stopped
collecting when she found Coltrane's recording on the
"Coltrane's Sound" album. After that there really wasn't
much more for her to know about the song and she made as
much peace with it as possible. It was a sad song about
longing for what you don't have and probably can't get.
She'd stopped singing it when she fell in love with Eddy Lee.
Or more exactly, no one asked her to sing it anymore; she was
too happy.

So it was very awful when she sang "Body and Soul"
that night. She had always sung it with the simple honesty of
a woman in love and now she sang it with that and the pain of
a woman whose lover had left her.

Alan had heard these lyrics before but they'd never
really meant much to him.

Nathan wished she'd go back to being cold and distant
in her singing. This was too much, too raw and painful to
watch.

Monty simply listened. There was no way to critique
this kind of singing, it was rare and beautiful and he was
merely glad he could still appreciate such sadness.

There was no applause after "Body and Soul" so the
band simply went on to the next song and the one after that
until they were done. Hackenbush was tired so she just
listened to the guys discussing the arrangements, which were
pretty straightforward, and the gig. Her father had a cigarette
and a cup of coffee and then asked her to walk him to his car.

"Nice job singing tonight, doc," he said, putting his stuff

in the backseat. "Sorry about Eddy."

"Yeah. I know you liked him, too."

"Men is strange creatures, doc," he said softly. "We don't always do the right thing the right way but sometimes it turns out to be that, dig?"

"Not really," she said, tapping a cigarette out of the pack in her hand. "Check back with me in six months; I might be able to understand it then."

He pinched her cheek and called her the maven maidela. "Go inside, hon, there's a serial killer on the loose," he said.

"This is a nice neighborhood, dad."

"He killed somebody in Mission Viejo and that's a nice neighborhood, too."

"Mission Viejo of all places; wow," she said. "I'll be careful. Drive safe; I'll see you tomorrow." Out of habit, she looked up and down the empty street for traffic and watched him drive away. She took one last puff and tossed her cigarette into the gutter. When she looked up she was face to face with a guy in raggedy clothes; she started but didn't scream.

"Spare change, lady?"

"Sorry, no. Smoke?" She offered him a cigarette and lit it for him.

"Thanks. Know a guy named Myron Cohen?" he asked.

"No, can't say I do," she lied.

"You see him, tell him I'm looking for him."

"And who might you be?"

"He'll know me when he sees me." He stepped around her and ambled down the deserted street.

She watched him go; looked away and when she looked back, he was gone. "Great. Now I'm hallucinating," she said and went in the house.

Hackenbush found a thoughtful Monty when she took his breakfast in the next morning.

"You do a good job protecting your father," he said over his eggs.

"I thought I was pretty rude to him." She sat at the end of the bed, sipping her breakfast Ramos Gin Fizz.

"Yes, my dear, so rude no one else (possibly someone

he'd even take seriously, like Ross or Cody) could be rude to him." Monty smiled at her. "Well done, brava, I must say."

She shrugged. "What can I tell ya? He is the only father I've got, however flawed."

"I think you ought to rethink your rendition of "Body and Soul", Mabel," he said a few bites later. "Either lower the intensity and let the song simply be a song or hand out razor blades and call it performance art. I know I wanted to open a vein last night."

"Oh pooh, Monty. I thought I did a fine job with it," she said, blowing a plume of smoke at the ceiling. "I think Alan and Nathan enjoyed it, too."

"Alan was rather quiet afterwards. Possibly he's starting to envision a life without me in it," Monty said.

"Let's hope he sees reason fairly soon," Hackenbush said and got up.

"I have a song for you to learn, Hackenbush," Monty told her as she picked up his breakfast tray. "It's called "Stardust" and it's on an old Keely Smith album."

"Sorry, not a fan of the lady or her husband."

"This is a solo album," he said. "You don't have to like the way she sings it to learn the song from her. Frankly, I don't care how you learn it, just learn it. It will make me happy to hear you sing it so just start learning it."

"Yes sir," she said and went into the kitchen to wash up. "Know a song called "Stardust", Cody?"

He sang a few words of the chorus, ending with "da da da dee dee dee. I only know the first line," he said.

"You guys know the first line of every song ever written," she said. "Monty wants me to learn it."

"It's a nice song," Ross said. "You'd probably get along with it, Mabel."

"Yeah, we'll see. I have to go to the Brand Library anyway, so I'll Xerox the music while I'm there. You guys need anything from there?" she asked and they said no as Shorty came in. "Know that song, "Stardust", Shorty?"

"No, but I'll go to the Brand with you," he said.

"Fine with me. What time do we leave for the gig? Seven?" she asked and was told that was so. She said she'd see them well before then and went into her day.

"I am going to hear Hackenbush tonight and I am wearing my tux and if you don't want to come, I'll take a cab." Monty was being firm with Alan. It was adorable, but not for Alan. "Oh, and I've called Nathan, so I hope your mood improves before he gets here."

"I'm sure Nathan has better things to do, Monty."

"He said he didn't," Monty remarked, digging around in his bureau.

"Wouldn't you like to have a quiet evening at home?"

"No, and you're in my light," Monty said, comparing shades of pancake make-up. "How dark do you think it will be in this place?"

"The last time I was in a bowling alley, it was fairly well lit," Alan said.

"What about the bar?"

"I was too young to go into the bar, Monty."

"Well, I'll go dark and hope for the best. I just want to cover these spots. Ah, there's Nathan, at last. We should give him a key," he said, rejecting sponges until he found one he liked.

"No, we shouldn't," Alan said, but answered the door anyway. After greeting his colleague, he got right to the point: "This is madness, Nathan, and he's not strong enough to go out like this."

"That's what I said. But he said he'd go without me, or us, if I didn't come," Nathan said, tossing his jacket on a chair. "Would he try to go alone?"

"Try and succeed probably."

"So... I wonder that he didn't go with the band then."

"Perhaps they said no, but I doubt that," Alan said, rubbing his temples. "No, I think this is just another maneuver to throw us together and for that I do apologize. Again."

"He is... irresistible, isn't he?"

"Yes. And now I must go find his tuxedo."

"Am I underdressed?" Nathan asked. He was wearing jeans, a plain t-shirt and a light-weight jacket.

"No, you and I are dressed appropriately for a bowling alley." Except for khaki trousers, Alan was dressed as casually as Nathan. "Or at least we'll be dressed like everyone else. But for Monty, the sartorial rules are a little different."

"Nathan! How delightful!" Monty, very and suddenly deeply tanned, wheeled himself into the room. "Have you found my tux, Alan?" he asked his boyfriend.

"Which one?"

"The dark blue brocade one, of course." Monty turned back to Nathan and suggested they order some Thai food while Alan was looking for his tux.

"So... do we know where we're going, Monty?" Nathan asked.

"Oh, somewhere off the Five freeway," Monty said, lighting a cigarette. "La Mirada can't be that hard to find. And then, there can only be one Lanes; I feel sure of that."

Nathan smiled politely and got the phone book.

Hackenbush had gone to her apartment earlier in the day, ostensibly to warm up and dress, but really to try to get over a terrible case of nerves. And not good, stage fright nerves; these were something different, something awful, something far too much like dread, despair and the horror of discovering that life really is a series of senseless and futile struggles that there's no way out of. Well, one way out, but it was so permanent. She felt great ugliness coming on and asked Shorty to take her car back to Monty's place.

"Sure you want to be alone, Mabel?" he asked, jingling her keys.

"Very sure. I'm never alone anymore." She looked around her stuffy, but tidy, little place.

"But it's been fun at Monty's, hasn't it?"

"Oh, yes; fun. We're playing beat the clock with Dr. Brazil's nerves and the Reaper, and I'm not sure who I'm betting on anymore," she said. "Tremendous fun! Hook it, Shorty; I have to warm up and commune with the song list before we go. Ask Ross or Cody to come get me for the gig, if they don't mind."

He said he would and left her alone with her thoughts.

Her thoughts were rather sorry to be left alone with her. Or rather, her thoughts were a little afraid of her emotions, which were dark, edgy and painful. They were the kind of emotions that cause people to immolate themselves just to get some relief. They were everything that make a loving woman who can no longer love the most dangerous creature on earth.

So, while her thoughts cowered in some far corner of her mind, she let her emotions spin out into all areas of her consciousness. She'd doped them with liquor and then with work, but they were still around—somewhat subdued but also somewhat rested from being ignored.

"Ah ha," her emotions made their presence known, as they ran their razors along her nerves. "We were quiet for a while, but now we're back. You can run, Hackenbush, but you can't hide. No one loves you, no one will ever love you and you will die alone. But first you will fail: yourself, others and, of course, society because what else can a fat, ugly, soon to be middle-aged single woman like you ever do but fail? You will never own a new car or a house or have a pension or health insurance or even a steady job. Really, Hackenbush, the most simple rube can get and hold down a job; why can't you? You make no contribution to anything, Hackenbush, you leave nothing behind you, no legacy, no monument, no impression, not even a shadow to show that you exist. And no one cares; why should they? What use are you to anyone, especially yourself? And you sure as hell can't pick 'em, can you? You put all your love and future into one guy and he leaves you. Doesn't even say good-bye, oh, wait, yes he did; let's play that message again, just to be sure it says the same thing it's been saying these past weeks. Yes, let's play it again, Hackenbush."

Her hand hovered over the answering machine as it occurred to her that it would be the same voice, saying the same things all over again and it might be better to just erase the tape.

"Coward," the voices said.

She pressed the rewind and then the play button. Eddy Lee's voice came over the tiny speaker: "Hi, Mabel, look, I gotta leave town for a while, y'know, we're like too hot not to cool down and I need to think about it for a while, maybe a long while, so, um, that's it, I'm done. Bye."

"Ah." The voices were satisfied.

"Ah, Eddy," she sighed, cueing the tape so it wouldn't

record over the message.

"Yes, Eddy; if he were here you could kill him," the voices said, somewhere around her hippocampus.

"I could, but probably wouldn't," she said, thinking it was a bad sign; living alone and talking out loud to the voices in your head.

"Yes, you would," the voices told her.

"No, it would be worse," she murmured. "I'd beg him to come back to me; it would be embarrassing, not lethal. Well, not in the physical sense."

"You could kill him and then yourself," the voices suggested.

"Oh please. How dramatic. It's bad enough without taking anyone with me."

"Coward," the voices said.

"Maybe." She glanced around the room for something sharp. "Maybe." How much damage can one do with a knife or razor? "Maybe." How do people kill themselves anyway? "Maybe." She didn't have a gun or a garage or... "Maybe." She had a bathtub and a hair dryer. "Maybe." How long would it really hurt? "Maybe." She looked over at her desk, thinking she should leave a note. At least let them know where to send the body. Nah. Her eye fell on a library book, an Inspector Maigret mystery.

One of the thoughts cowering in her brain tugged at her. She opened the book and looked at the due date. It was overdue; way overdue.

"OH MY GOD!" Hackenbush grabbed for her car keys, which Shorty had along with the car, and not finding them, flung her purse away from her. And then lunged for it; she'd need money. Clutching the overdue book to her chest, she ran out the door and down the hill to the local library.

If anyone thought it was strange to see a soon to be middle-aged white woman running like a lunatic with a book in her arms, they did not mention it. They were just lucky they couldn't see it from her side.

By the time she got to the library, she'd pretty much outrun her panic. She paid her fine, checked out a Simenon book she hadn't read and said hi to one of the clerks she knew. On her way home, she took a small detour and walked around the Echo Park lake. It was crowded that Saturday; it was always crowded when the weather was warm.

She stopped at the tiny market near the lake and bought some cigarettes. She wished they had more than a beer and wine license, but if she really wanted the hard stuff, she could walk up to Sunset and get it. She was too tired, she was too numb to get any more numb; so she took her cigarettes and went home.

At home, hot as it was, she closed her windows. She turned on the TV, the radio, put on a record of Coltrane and Dolphy playing "My Favorite Things" live at Newport and all very loud. This recording went on and on and on and Hackenbush sang every verse as loud as she could. She played it over and over, until she was worn out and warmed up. She would rest up for the gig on the way there. She hoped Cody or Ross would be on the early side to pick her up.

Depending on traffic, the drive to La Mirada is either long or short. The Five freeway south that evening was quiet for the Five. Even so, Cody spent far too much time in second gear to be happy about it. "I'm starting to agree with your father about LA traffic," he said.

Hackenbush lit another cigarette and stared out the window. "This is why daddy and I almost never visit each other." She pointed at the northbound side of the freeway. "Notice that the traffic going back to LA is flying; we're just heading in the wrong direction. Story of my life."

Cody glanced at her but didn't say anything. She was in an odd mood, he could tell, and not her usual keyed up nervous pre-gig mood. That mood he liked, it meant there would be fine music made and much happiness reaped. This mood was unfamiliar to him; dark, bitter and ugly about life in general. She'd been quiet most of the ride, her few remarks were gloomy and sarcastic lacking her usual wit. He was undecided whether he should just ignore it and let her work it out or if he should provoke her and let her get it out of her system before they got anywhere near the gig. Cody was a brave man, but taking a sidelong look at the set of her shoulders and pinched profile, he decided to let her work it out. By the look of her, she might decide to grab the wheel and ram the van across the freeway divider if he annoyed her.

Not that that hadn't occurred to Hackenbush at least once on the ride. That or drive them off a cliff, but there were no cliffs on that stretch of the Five. This was proof to her that she'd only eluded her self-destructive mood of earlier in the day and if Cody wasn't driving, she couldn't say what might have happened on the trip to La Mirada. In fact, this drive to La Mirada was turning into something of a quest for her, an endurance trial of sorts; she wondered if she'd survive it or just sink lower and lower and finally implode into her mood, leaving poor Cody to sweep her ashes off his passenger seat. Perhaps she'd save the imploding for the gig. No; dying on stage might be swell, but at the La Mirada Lanes? No. Only if she could take out a few bowlers while she was at it; otherwise, no. Long, powerful brown fingers snapping in front of her face brought her back to the present.

"Hackenbush, we're here."

She looked at the faded, peeling structure before her in the Orange County twilight and frowned. "Oh, my Lord, are we ever," she sighed and got out of the van. "Why are we doing this again, Cody?" she asked, picking up his music stand.

"Something to do with Ross and Moody, I think," Cody said, locking the van up. "I mean, what else have we got to do tonight?"

"Aside from slitting my throat, nothing I can think of," she thought and then seeing Cody's shocked face, realized she'd said it out loud. "Ha ha! Just kidding, darlin', just kidding, ha-ha-ha." She flashed her brightest smile into his unconvinced face and breezed past him to open the smeary glass door.

Cubic square miles of cigarette smoke over years and years had finally permeated the air conditioning system of the La Mirada Lanes. There was a cool, gritty, almost mentholated, feel to the air that greeted the singer and bassist as they stepped into the lobby where the shoe rental was to the right and the lounge was to the left. Hackenbush found herself rubbing her fingers over her cheeks, trying to wipe off a layer of powdery grime being blown on her from the huge vents in the lobby. A fine, dry and invisible dust seemed to settle all over her, weighing her down, marking her place, and it took her a moment to realize that it was the mood of the La Mirada Lanes settling over her more than any real substance. She cast a sidelong glance at Cody, trudging along beside her, and didn't see any of the mood on him. He was looking around at the lanes and the snack bar, so she did, too, and also realized that he was the only black person in the whole huge expanse of the place. Once they got into the lounge, they found Shorty and Ross had already arrived. Ross was setting up and he looked relieved to see them.

"We're the only Negroes in here," he said to Cody. "Hi, Mabel."

"Well, they didn't stare too hard when we came in," Cody said with a grim smile. "They did stare, but I think it was at Hackenbush."

"Only because they've never seen this much charm in one place," she said, flashing another brilliant fake smile at them.

"Doesn't that hurt your face?" Ross asked.

"You know... it does." She rubbed her cheek.

"Then stop it, or save it for the bowlers," he growled. "Oh, there's Moody." He waved; he had a wry, 'it's-not-really-my-fault' smile on his face as he did so.

Mabel turned to look and smiled reflexively and defensively to keep the stupid stunned look off her face. This was the fattest, whitest white guy she'd ever seen in her life.

He was huge; almost as wide as he was tall. "Is it glandular?" she hissed at Ross.

"Nah, just trying to eat himself to death," Ross hissed back.

"Like Elvis?" Shorty asked in stunned whisper. He, too, had a stunned smile frozen on his face. "Didn't Elvis...?" he began when they all just stared at him.

"I wouldn't know," Hackenbush snapped and turned her attention to being introduced to John Moody. He raked his light blue eyes over her and pushed his colorless hair off his forehead. He might have said hello but to Hackenbush it sounded like he might have just cleared his throat. She smiled because she didn't know what else to do. He didn't smile or even look at her again.

"I'll need two of those chairs." He grunted and jerked his chin at the armless straight backed bar chairs. He turned his back on her and hoisted his amp onto the stage.

Glad to be ignored, Hackenbush and Shorty collected two chairs and handed them up onto the stage. By then the rest of the band was arriving and they removed themselves to watch from a discreet distance.

Hackenbush had grown up around these guys so each one came over and hugged her. As politely as her mood would allow her to, she introduced them all to Shorty as Uncle Whomever.

She was still in an ugly, edgy, alienated, depressed kind of mood. Almost as if she'd rather not sing at all, a dark and inert mood that might or might not be communicable.

Shorty noticed and tried to jolly her out of it with a drink. Unfortunately the bar only stocked beer and wine, and Hackenbush loathed both. He brought her a Coke instead and she was reasonably content with that. "We ought to carry a flask for emergencies, Mabel," Shorty said.

"And get hauled in for an open container in a moving vehicle violation? I think not, Shorty," she snarled.

"Well then, darling, next time we play a bowling alley, let's call ahead and find out what the booze situation is," he said rather sourly. Her mood was catching and his resistance was down.

"There will be no next time, pal," she said, glancing around at the Naugahyde furnishings and scuffed linoleum floor. A dance floor of sorts. The whole floor was linoleum, thus making the room very boomy. She might as well not use the PA since she could bounce her voice off the floor, the glass walls and Formica table tops. "I'm in hell," she thought. "This is where the unsuccessful end up; trying to sing over the crash and roar of strikes, splits and whatever other fucking bowling noise they have in hell."

To distract herself and feel useful, Hackenbush took her baritone ukulele out and tuned it. She looked up into Moody's eyes, watching her; she smiled politely and he played A440 for her and the band to tune to. Hackenbush didn't have absolute pitch (just good relative pitch), but it sounded like A440 to her. Since they weren't tuning to a piano, they'd have to trust Moody's ear for pitch.

Hackenbush was watching Moody watching her. If she'd been in a different frame of mind and he were several dozen pounds lighter, well, sparks might have flown. He had that frank stare and bad attitude she might have found attractive if she didn't now hate all men, except the ones she knew and liked. As it was, she was merely sizing him up as either an accompanist or an opponent—either would do this evening, since it was doomed ('doomed,' she told herself), completely doomed, what did it matter how they played? If they made music together? If the audience was in on the joke? If there was any joke at all? Likely, with the mood she was in and the general state of the Hackenbushian universe, she and Moody would simply skin strips of skin off of each other, scraping the fat away, until the exposed underlying muscle turned as hard as beef jerky and the floor opened and they were all sucked into a fiery pit and never seen again. And that was the best possible outcome for the evening.

These ruminations were interrupted by a very middle-aged woman with a tawny blonde dye job that was grey at the roots grabbing Hackenbush and getting lipstick all over her right cheek. "Little Miss Mabel! You're adorable! Look how big you are!"

"Oh, hi Aunt Marie," Hackenbush said, smearing the fuchsia smear further over her profile. Hackenbush waved at Uncle Phil, Marie's pianist husband, getting them drinks at the bar. She liked her faux Auntie, who was a sweetie and a wonderful vibes player, too. Marie and Phil were two of Louis' more reliable friends and always happy to baby-sit young Mabel. They thought she was the greatest thing that ever happened. Hackenbush read somewhere that if you have at least one person who thinks you are the greatest thing that ever happened, then the chances of becoming a sociopath were reduced by at least fifty percent. Or was it five percent? Well, didn't matter; Hackenbush had Aunt Marie and Uncle Phil, so she figured she was pretty damn safe from becoming a sociopath. "It's really nice of you to come hear us in this, um, bowling alley."

"Baby, a gig's a gig. And you don't sing in my neighborhood too often, so I gotta take my spots where I can get 'em." Marie smiled warmly at her and then frowned a little. "Listen, honey, I heard what that son of a bitch Eddy Lee did to you, that low-life motherfucker, if he was here or I knew where he was, I'd rip his fucking guts out and eat them in front of him."

Hackenbush nodded pleasantly at these savage remarks and smiled affectionately at her Auntie. "Gee, that sounds great, Aunt Marie" she sighed. "I wish he was here or I knew where he was so I could watch."

"I'd love that, honey. Is this young fella your new boyfriend?" Marie asked, glaring at Shorty standing politely beside Hackenbush.

"Well, no, not mine," Hackenbush said, making introductions. "We dance together; you'll see. Hi, Uncle Phil," she mumbled against his checked sports coat as he crushed her in a one-armed bearhug.

"Howya, doc!" he rumbled, hugging her a little closer.

"Good... good," she gasped, trying to expand her lungs enough to get a full breath. She sucked in a lungful of air when he finally let her go. She introduced him to Shorty and watched them manfully shake hands.

The macho transformation straight older men inspired in Shorty never failed to fascinate Hackenbush. In many ways Shorty was more feminine than she was, however, just now he standing with his legs spread wider than usual, his arms folded in front of him and nodding—his jaw cocked at a surly angle—listening manfully to whatever Uncle Phil and Uncle Martin, who'd just joined them, were saying. Hackenbush receded into the silent passivity that women allow themselves to recede into when the men are talking. It was kind of a relief and a novelty; usually she had to hold up her end of the conversation, but not here and not now. So she just listened and greeted the other Aunts and Uncles that rushed up to maul her. She loved these folks and they loved her; she'd miss it if they didn't grab her and exclaim about how big she was now. It would destroy one of the few traditions in her haphazard, lackadaisical and come-what-may way of life.

Her father had a few traditions, too, and one of them was to arrive right before the gig started so he wouldn't have to help set up. Well, that was Louis for you, and there he was.

Yes, there he was and there was a strange woman on his arm. At least she was one Hackenbush had never seen before, but she certainly fit the pattern. Bad dye-job on the hair, too much make-up on the face and trying to fit into a size smaller than her fat really wanted to fit into. Hackenbush figured that Louis was just getting too old and weird to catch pretty women anymore; at least the ones he got now were striking in their own bizarre ways. All she could hope was that Louis didn't expect her to have a conversation with his new babe. Hackenbush might have to ask her where she bought her make-up trowels. So she was relieved when Louis simply waved at her on his way to the bandstand and started to unpack his clarinet.

The little group around Hackenbush spread out, trying to make it look like a bigger crowd, and she excused herself to go fix up her face, which had several shades of new lipstick on it and none of them hers. On her way to the ladies room, she passed her father's new girlfriend and was flummoxed to see her applying even more make-up. 'What does she take it off with? A sandblaster?' Hackenbush wondered on her way by.

After scraping off her aunties' lipstick and applying a light coat of powder and freshening her own paint job, Hackenbush felt up to braving the sparse bar crowd. She heard the band start up and decided to brush her hair for a while. She had just gotten almost to the bar entrance when Moody started his solo, which hit her in the solar plexus and nearly knocked her down. There was a convenient wall to lean on and a few shadows to recover in. If the bowlers thought she was drunk, they could fuck off and die. She was reeling from the purity of Moody's playing; the tone, the phrasing, the silences were exquisite. She was glad she wasn't where Moody could see her; she wouldn't mind telling him how much she liked his playing, but he might consider it indiscreet to see it tearing her apart in front of God and everyone.

For Hackenbush it was also sad to hear such beautiful playing when all it did was remind her of Eddy Lee, whom she'd probably never see again. Moody's playing was not like Eddy's, but it had the same wistful, cocky spirit and

Hackenbush fought back her tears because she didn't want to have to fix her make-up again. And the idea of crying in the La Mirada Lanes was far too humiliating.

And then it was over and her father was soloing in his heavy-handed way. Louis had been playing pretty much the same solo ever since she could remember, so she used the opportunity to take a deep breath and pull herself together. One of the bowlers leered at her on his way into the bar; staring him down plunked her back down to earth and very much back into the present. She went into the bar and found Shorty at the same table, looking dazed but happy. He very subtly jerked his chin in Moody's direction and smiled.

Hackenbush smiled coolly and let her smile become much more of a sneer when she looked at Moody, who was watching her as she suspected. She tilted her chin at him in recognition and looked away before his smoldering, but empty, look unnerved her. It was that look musicians get when they're simultaneously looking somebody over in the audience and listening to the rest of the band. She knew she had that look when she was on the stand, but never liked it directed at her. Of course, she and Moody were already in a war of nerves, so anything could happen and it was only the first set.

'We're perfect for each other,' she thought. 'He's been burned and hates women; I've been burned and hate men. He could crush me to death during sex and that would also be perfect.' She turned her head and noticed Shorty's lips were moving. "What?" she asked, leaning toward him.

Shorty pressed his lips against her ear. "Where does your dad get these sax players?"

Hackenbush glanced over at the tenor player mutilating the song and then at Cody, Ross and Moody, who all had the 'oh, Lord, just let me survive the next eight bars' look on their faces. "That's Uncle Bob, Shorty," she said, as if this were enough answer for anyone.

"He sucks, Mabel."

She lit a cigarette to buy her a little time to dredge up a good answer. "I think he's not warmed up yet," she said, picking a piece of tobacco off her tongue. She cast a sidelong glance at him to see if he was buying it and could see he was not. However, he said nothing as she politely applauded Uncle Bob's pathetic solo and exchanged another sneer with Moody.

"He can't take his eyes off of you," Shorty said, rising for their dance number.

"Who?"

"Moody, silly."

"How do you know he's not staring at you?" she asked sweetly but never got an answer because they glided onto the empty space in front of the band and danced a chorus.

They danced beautifully even though the floor, the sound, the lighting—the entire situation—could have been better, but still, they were their usual delightful selves. Little Mabel's fans gave them a round of applause; the smattering of bowlers simply stared at them in horror.

"Um..." Shorty began.

"Yeah, well, that might be enough dancing until, um... something," Hackenbush said, trying not to let the blank stares rattle her too badly. 'I'm dancing with Shorty in the bowling alley of the damned; oh where have I sinned to deserve this?' she asked herself. She smiled back at Aunt Marie's wink and thumbs up and wished she had something stronger than a Coke to drink.

The song ended and another started. Moody broke her heart again (but she hid it); her father bored her (but she pretended to be fascinated) and the rest of the band dragged itself through the poor, defenseless tune that Ross and Cody kept going out of pure will or pure orneriness or both. Very charmingly, Cody tilted his chin at the entrance and Hackenbush twisted around to see who'd come in. Well, of course, it was her favorite gay triangle arriving in style. "What's that thing Monty says about men in tuxedos?" she asked Shorty.

"He's magnificent, Mabel, just face it!"

Probably the La Mirada Lanes had not seen a midnight blue brocade tuxedo in living memory, so Hackenbush was glad she was able to witness this historic event. She was even gladder when Monty hauled out a thermos full of gimlets and poured her one. "I see you've brought proper provisions for this expedition, Monty," she murmured.

"It's a bowling alley, my dear; even if they were willing to make a gimlet, they'd likely not have the kind of gin I like." He fitted one of her cigarettes into his holder and leaned back, smoking and listening pensively. "What a motley crew, Hackenbush; only Cody and Ross are at all attractive up there."

"Really? Don't you find Uncle Al, playing the trombone over there, somewhat nice looking?" she asked over the rim of her drink.

"Possibly fifteen years ago and in the dark."

Hackenbush didn't answer; she smiled at Albany and Brazil, who'd come back from the bar with beers. Of the five of them at that table, she and the pair 'o docs were by far the most manly. But there was hint of hostility from the direction of the bar, so even Shorty and Monty were being low-key and rather butch. Hackenbush suspected their dancing had jolted some sensibilities she could not (and did not want to) understand. Or maybe it was just fashion: she was wearing a smart black dress cut just below her knees and loose enough to dance and sing in, but fitted in all the right places show off her curves and hide the bulges; Shorty was wearing a mustard colored suit and a pink bow tie. Was that enough to annoy the natives? Well, probably; or perhaps the locals simply didn't like loudly dressed men in their bowling alleys. Looking over the dazzling array of bowling shirts at the bar, Hackenbush could understand why that might be so. One more dazzling color in this room and they'd all go blind.

On the other hand, maybe these guys and gals at the bar had had a bad day, or were losing at bowling (however one did that), or didn't like the music, or were just naturally pissed off. Hackenbush met the naturally pissed off all the time on temp jobs; they were everywhere and usually originally had good reasons to be pissed off. However, because they never did anything to get un-pissed-off, well, their pissed-off-ness had become like those scars drunks get, and can't remember how they got them, but were damn sure it was someone else's fault. And thereby became naturally pissed off and would feel naked without it. So to hell with them.

Hackenbush's ruminations had gone on for so long and so deeply, she almost missed her father's introduction. When

Shorty jabbed her, she only caught "... direct from the middle class, my little girl, the fabulous Dr. Hackenbush!"

With a dazzling smile, she grabbed her baritone ukulele and dashed up to the stand. She reached for the mike, but her father held onto it.

"Here to sing 'Body and Soul' for you tonight!" Louis added, handing her the microphone.

Hackenbush's dazzling smile froze as she thought, 'Oh shit.' She glanced back at Ross and Cody, who groaned softly in sympathy. Possibly Moody picked up the vibe because, incredibly, his sneer deepened as he looked up at her with his pale, empty eyes. He nodded at her and played a very hip four bar intro.

Hackenbush took a breath and was about to launch into her tragic lament when there was a strike or something loud and a lot of happy commotion in the lanes. The sound died in her throat as she watched a minor stampede from the bar to the windows overlooking the lanes. There was some shouting, growling and fist shaking that she didn't understand and wasn't meant to understand anyway. The band waited for the mob to settle down; better not to play, it would only annoy or enrage them. Hackenbush exchanged an arch look with Monty; Shorty and the docs were very still next to him.

Still poised on the verge of her song, Hackenbush looked back into Moody's eyes. She might have been reading him wrong, but he seemed to be waiting for her to fail, to fall flat on her ass, to irritate at least fifty percent of her audience when her job was to entertain, if not entrance them. And here she was, about to sing some serious, tragic jazz in a bowling alley and all she wanted to do was slap the smirk off fatboy's face.

All this passed in a heartbeat and, never breaking eye contact with Moody, Hackenbush patted the top of her head and growled, "Me and Moody; jump in where you can, cats." Snapping her fingers, she counted off the time and set them off into the country stomp version of "Body and Soul."

She could feel the shock go through the band behind her as she sang but she kept looking at Moody. She knew that if she looked at Shorty or Monty, they would have that stunned look on their faces, so she just kept looking at Moody. Had she looked at Aunt Marie and the other aging hipsters they would be puzzled but adoring, so she went on looking at Moody. And if she'd turned her head, she'd have seen several pairs of bowlers dancing some weird two-step in front of the stand, but she just kept looking at Moody, who was the only other sentient being in the whole fucking universe who got the joke.

Ross and Cody were laying down perfectly competent county western dance licks, but she could feel them feeling their way along this bizarre version of "Body and Soul" she was cantering through. Once they'd decided she might be onto something good, the horn players found a groove then came along for the ride. Only Moody was really with her, comping along, supporting her so-square-it's-hip rendition of the song and even adding a few guitar quotes she thought she'd heard Roy Owens (or was it Buck Clark?) play on Hee Haw in those seconds before anyone could get to the TV to change the channel.

But it was working and the room was in love with them before the first chorus ended. One of the bowlers, obviously a man of taste and refinement, very gallantly bowed and offered her his hand. Well, what the hell? Hackenbush put down her ukulele and allowed herself to be led off the stage and into a hybrid polka swing sort of dance. It must have been their lucky night because for two people who'd never danced together, they made it look pretty good.

Hackenbush glanced over her partner's royal blue shoulder and saw that everyone, except Monty, was dancing. Probably the women had grabbed all the stray men, including Albany, Brazil and Shorty and dragged them onto the dance floor. It was wild; Albany and Brazil looked like pretty good dancers, it would be nice to see them dance together (but, please God, not here). She caught her father's eye and whirled her index finger over her head to make him keep it going. He winked back and made the same gesture to the band. The other thing she noticed was Moody watching her without a sneer, simply watched her the way a guitar player watches a pretty lady on the dance floor. It was a normal and reassuring look. And a grateful look; Hackenbush had the crowd eating out of her hand, the band could have played

"The Rite of Spring" and gotten away with it, as long as everyone could keep dancing.

But all good things come to an end and eventually Hackenbush dislodged herself from her partner's arms and returned to the bandstand. She went early to catch her breath and then sang the last chorus in a way that would have gotten her a standing ovation in any bowling alley in the universe. And did. When the applause died down, she decided to see what she could do to "I Got it Bad and That Ain't Good." It was magnificent, so magnificent that they were all worn out and took a well-deserved break.

Moody caught her left hand and brought it to his lips. She smiled at him and leaned down to hear what he said.

"You're a fucking genius, Dr. Hackenbush," he said, dropping her hand.

"You, too, Mr. Moody; you, too."

Hackenbush pretty much had the audience in her pocket the rest of the evening. To be on the safe side, she and the band stuck to danceable tunes and she and Shorty didn't dance. They didn't dance with each other, but they danced their legs to stumps with other people. The crowd might be hipper than when they came in, but they were miles from being hip enough to tolerate, let alone appreciate, Hackenbush and Shorty tripping the light fantastic. So they didn't bother to trip anything. They did wind up dancing a modified hustle to a souped-up "There Will Never be Another You," which somehow seemed appropriate.

And the night ground on and on. Hackenbush sang competently, but her heart wasn't in it; her heart was nowhere near it. She thought Moody played like a dream, maybe even better than Eddy Lee, but she would be glad to be away from him. It seemed to her that the moment he stopped waiting for her to fail, he began waiting for her to transcend reality for him. Well, even if she could, it hardly seemed like the right thing to do on their first gig. And he seemed like the kind of guy who'd ask you to walk on water, and then when you did, he'd want you to dance on it, too. Hackenbush felt bound to disappoint the poor bastard; better let her memory gracefully fade away in his mind than have her all-too-humanness bring him down. God knew it brought her down enough as it was.

Yeah, it wasn't a bad night. Ross and Cody seemed amused by the old white cats scene her father collected around him. They got to swing with Moody, whom they liked very much, and the three of them slipped in snide little riffs under the clunky solos. But they were all business when Hackenbush sang. Because of her earlier success in bringing out the best in a potentially ugly crowd, they let her set the tone of each song and then they improved upon it. This impressed her, and it impressed them that it impressed her.

Monty was having a good time. He watched the action on the bandstand like it was a chess match. He felt Hackenbush and Moody were putting on a show all for him. And the music, contorted though it was to fit the situation, was enjoyable. Hackenbush had a lovely voice and a graceful stage presence; too bad her presence stopped at the edge of the stage tonight. She and Moody were a pair; both brilliant, but hard and distant up there on the stage. If Monty closed his eyes, the singer and guitarist cast a warmer glow over the room. But watching them was not very much fun; Monty had seen plastic flamingos with more charisma.

But possibly he had unrealistic expectations. This was not his living room, and Hackenbush was up against a culture she was unfamiliar with and obviously uncomfortable in; perhaps he ought to give the girl a break. No, a diamond shines in any setting; she'd just have to stop being fussy and get on with her art. The other bar patrons noticed none of this; they were busy drinking and dancing and generally having a good time. Monty allowed himself to enjoy their pleasure. He was also enjoying watching Alan and Nathan having fun in spite of themselves.

Now, those two docs danced and chatted with a continuous stream of heavily made up, heavyset and very middle aged women. Some were good dancers, some were not, but Alan and Nathan brought out the best in each of them. Even Hackenbush noticed this and cursed her sex for being prettier, smarter, livelier under an admiring male gaze, even an admiring fag gaze. But there you had it; somewhere in life Alan and Nathan had learned to be nice to a certain kind of women. The kind that had exactly zero impact on them beyond the present moment. And there they were, dancing, chatting and even charming these frowsy broads right here in front of God and everyone in the fabulous La Mirada Lanes.

But all things end eventually and soon they had the vans packed up and were saying good-night all. Hackenbush's father pulled her aside and told her which Norm's coffee shop they were heading for. She smiled warmly at him; he'd chosen Norm's because she liked it—he'd taken her to Norm's for her sweet sixteen dinner with Dad—so it had meaning for both of them. This touching father-daughter moment was slashed up by gunshots, screaming and squealing tires roaring away into the night. Father and daughter cautiously looked around the end of Cody's van and saw Drs Albany and Brazil running toward two guys crawling around in their own blood.

Hackenbush found Ross in the crowd and dragged him along with her. "Gimme your keys, pal," she said, holding out her hand. "See you at Norm's." She waved as he and Cody drove away in Cody's van.

Very quickly, she collected Shorty and found Monty looking rather distressed by the scene and put him in Ross's van as well. She pulled up next to Moody as he looked on with the crowd at the first aid in progress. "Coming to Norm's with us, Mr. Moody?" she asked, leaning out the window.

"Nah, think I'll see how this show shakes out," he said, giving her that cocky appraising look she'd seen all evening. He added a smile and that was kind of nice. "I'll tell your friends where you went when the cops get done with 'em."

"Much obliged, brother, much obliged," she said and pulled into traffic as the sirens started to wail.

An hour later, Albany and Brazil finished giving the police their statement, which was minimal because they hadn't seen anything until the shooting was over. They went back inside and washed the blood off their hands; there was nothing they could do about their clothes. The bartender asked them to have one on the house, so they went back into the bar, where they found Moody waiting for them.

"Hackenbush took your pal in the wheelchair with her to Norm's," he said and gave them directions.

Albany and Brazil exchanged exhausted looks and decided to just go home after all this. They thanked him and finished their drinks.

"What you think of Miss Dr. Hackenbush?" Moody asked as they were leaving.

"I think she's trouble," Brazil snarled. He was very tired and wished he was already home.

"All women are trouble," Moody said. "What else is new?" He picked up his guitar and left without another word.

Brazil looked away from Moody's back and back at Albany, who said, "Let's go."

In the car on the way home, Albany started to laugh. He had a warm and good-natured laugh. It was infectious, too, because very soon Brazil was laughing with him.

"What are we laughing about, Nathan?" he asked when he was able to.

"That Miss Dr. Hackenbush probably is trouble," Albany said with a cheerful weariness Brazil had never heard before. "That tonight was bizarre and uncomfortable, but... but not unpleasant, and that I can't remember ever being this happy before."

"I think you're exhausted," Brazil said firmly. "I know I am. I haven't danced or done so much first aid in many many years."

"Well... the dancing was all right. Not much we could do for first aid except try to keep the bleeding under control until the paramedics arrived."

"Yes, well, I guess it was better than nothing," Brazil said vaguely.

"Oh, it was much better than nothing, Alan; you're a wonderful doctor," Albany said warmly and quickly for him.

"And all my patients die," Brazil thought but simply said, "Thank you, you were great, too," and drove on in silence.

Traffic was light except where CalTrans was setting up shop, and then they only had one lane closed, so it wasn't as bad as it could have been.

"I think you're too tired to drive, Nathan," Brazil said when they got to his place. "I think you should stay here tonight."

Albany dearly hoped this wasn't a come-on because if he was too tried to drive... "I... I wouldn't want to inconvenience you, Alan."

"You won't; you can sleep in the guest room."

"Where will you sleep?"

"In Monty's room; he used to be used to it, I'm sure he can cope for one night," Brazil said, leading his houseguest in and settling him in the guest room.

Meanwhile at Norm's, Hackenbush, Ross, Cody, Shorty, Monty and Louis were quite comfortable in the big corner booth. No one else turned up, not even Louis' current girlfriend, and a relieved Hackenbush didn't ask any questions, so they went ahead and ordered. They were starving because the food in the vending machines at the bowling alley had not appealed to them.

"That was quite a culture clash," Monty said once he'd quelled the worst hunger pangs with some soft-boiled eggs and toast.

Hackenbush, seated between Monty and her father, looked up from her steak but kept her mouth shut.

"Oh? How so?" Louis asked, lighting up while people were still eating as usual.

"Your lovely daughter hardly fits into a bowling alley, Mr. Hackenbush, I'm sure you agree," Monty drawled, lighting one of Mabel's cigarettes.

"She did all right," Louis said, draping his arm around Mabel. "People just want to dance and have a good time. We managed to give them that tonight, didn't we baby?"

Hackenbush just smiled at him; this was the answer he liked best.

"I think those people would have been happy with a jukebox and some disco lights," Cody said.

"Yeah, I don't think we added anything to anyone's life tonight," Ross said.

"Just my point, gentlemen, there was no common ground tonight. Hackenbush bridged it by going into unfamiliar territory for her, but vaguely familiar to everyone in the room," Monty said, sipping his coffee. It was awful coffee; he made a face and put it aside. "You could have been singing anything in that rocking horse rhythm you got into, Hackenbush; as long as people could feel the time in their guts and feet they were happy. You lulled them into a sense of security, you could have danced them off a cliff. That makes you an even more dangerous woman than I'd thought."

"Oh, please, Monty," Hackenbush sighed, giving up on her steak and lighting a cigarette. "I just didn't want to rip my guts for no reason. All that would have done was annoy the crowd. Seemed to me that they were folks that just wanted to relax and enjoy their evening after a long day at work. The last thing they want is me up there, howling about lost love and how fucked up my life is from it."

"But that would have been familiar, too, Hackenbush," Monty persisted. "We all suffer from love at least once or twice in life; why didn't you try to touch that chord tonight? I know you can; I've seen you do it."

"Because it wouldn't have been appropriate for the situation," she said primly.

"Nonsense."

"Okay, I'm a coward," she sighed. "And Moody was making me really fucking nervous." She glared at Ross. "What's with that guy?"

"He always gives singers a hard time, Mabel," Ross said. "You passed the Moody test tonight though."

"Fucking bully for me," she snarled. "I wrecked several perfectly good songs, I disco danced and I was ironic and I loathe irony."

"I adore irony! What don't you like about it?" Monty asked.

"Like sarcasm, it's too easy to ignore or misinterpret," she said, fumbling around in her thoughts. She knew she didn't like irony or sarcasm but had never had to explain why. "Irony is a waste of time. If you got something to say, fucking say it; don't hide behind some asshole attitude that you use to wiggle out of what you said by saying it's not what you meant. Dig?"

"Sort of," Shorty said.

"And yet you were quite ironic this evening, my dear, why was that?" Monty asked.

"I just wanted to get through the evening in one piece," she said. "I wanted them to like me, but I wanted it to be okay if they didn't like me."

"Oh, honey, everybody loves you," Louis said vaguely.

He hadn't really been listening, but could hear the stress in his little girl's voice.

"Yeah, right, daddy," she laughed. "Seriously, Monty, usually I don't care what the audience thinks, but tonight I was in a room full of people who were indifferent or hostile and it mattered. I just wanted to lay low, get it over with and get out. A deeply and very weird feeling."

"Welcome to the modern world, my dear," Monty said, exchanging knowing looks with Shorty, Ross and Cody. "Being a white, straight, female was once respectable enough; now if your ideology or fashion strays from children-kitchen-church, you're a pariah-outlaw-deviant danger to society and will be viewed with suspicion and hatred all your days."

"God, Monty, do I get a leper bell to go with the outfit?" she asked in mock horror, stubbing her cigarette out.

"Was that irony, Mabel?" Shorty asked, winking at her.

"Just a little; sorry," she said. "So, Ross, tell me about Moody. I'm in love with his playing."

"He's a monster," Ross said admiringly. "Too bad he doesn't get out more."

"Well, if he lost some weight and got a haircut–"

"There's more to it than that, Mabel," Ross cut her off. "Moody got hurt. I guess we all assume it was a woman—usually is, and don't frown at me like that—but it was more than that. It was like his whole life collapsed, like he thought he was in heaven and when he found out he was on earth, well, no point in leaving the house anymore. So he stays home, out of trouble, and plays the guitar and figures he doesn't need anything else."

"Maybe he doesn't," she said, lighting another cigarette for herself and one for Monty. "I'd stay home and sing all day if I could afford it. I have to go to work and support myself."

"I don't know what he lives on," Ross said. "And, Mabel, you like an audience too much to stay home and sing with the radio."

"Ain't that the truth," Louis laughed. He leaned back and lit a cigarette.

"But about Moody," Ross continued. "He just doesn't want to be bothered with trying to be what other people want him to be. Like a certain white girl singer who thinks he should lose weight and get a haircut."

"Okay, okay, I'm a jerk; I admit it," she sighed.

"No, not a jerk," Monty said quietly. "I'd say you're just still trying to get along with a society that doesn't want to get along with you anymore. If it ever did." He puffed his smoke. "You haven't opted for isolation, yet, and you know what Fellini said about isolation."

"I've no idea what Fellini said about isolation, Monty," Hackenbush said coolly.

"Well, Fellini's early films were, in part, studies on the subject of loneliness and observations of isolated persons, the out-of-step, those people who didn't fit in for one reason or another. He thought that it was usually people who are either too smart or are too stupid who are left out of the mainstream. The difference is, the smart ones often isolate themselves, while the less intelligent ones are usually isolated by the others. In *Nights of Cabiria*, I think he said, he was exploring the pride of one of those who has been excluded," Monty said. "Moody has excluded himself for his own set of reasons. And tonight, Hackenbush, you withheld yourself for other reasons. And you, Ross, Cody and Shorty, you all banked your fires and withdrew into yourselves in self defense. The law of our time is fit in or be destroyed and those that can't or won't fit in suffer at the hands of those who do."

"Maybe in France, but that's not how it is here," Louis said sounding rather offended.

"In theory, yes; in practice, no, Mr. Hackenbush," Monty said pleasantly. "At least Reagan and his gang are callous or honest or arrogant or whatever enough to disregard the trappings of compassion and understanding of those different from themselves for the reality of how they would and now are running the country. The strong rule now and the weak hope for a few crumbs."

"It's always been like that, Monty," Ross said quietly.

"Ross, I believe you're a few years younger than me and you might not remember as much of the past as I do," Monty said, smiling grimly. "I can recall a time when we were a country that was striving to eradicate poverty and ignorance and injustice. We were once governed by white men who could actually see another's point of view. Who could look on the unsuccessful, the different, the other with true compassion and not contempt. Who could actually want those people to succeed simply because it was the right thing to want. Who could see more than a bank balance and a net worth. All we have left of that dream is Head Start, and the Reagan administration is still trying to get rid of it in the belief that all the waste in government is in the programs that help the most helpless and therefore those who will be the least able to defend themselves. We are now governed by men who believe poverty, plague and despair are lifestyle choices instead of the misfortune of living in a society that runs on fear and greed. This is a sad and terrible end for the country that created the polio vaccine, tin foil and Gene Kelly, but there you have it."

"Criticizing the country like that isn't very patriotic," Louis said stiffly.

"My dear Mr. Hackenbush, sometimes the truest patriotism is seeing your country for what it is and loving it anyway, warts and all." Monty smiled charmingly. "I will be giving up my illusion that we still stand for something aside from avarice and arrogance, but we don't and haven't for a long time. When we are told that our biggest enemy is the Soviet Union, that Evil Empire, and most of the country buys it because it'd be too much trouble to turn off the TV and look out the window and see that the true enemy, the true evil is poverty, disease, greed and decay, all of which we have in abundance once you step outside of the country club. This is not going to go away by ignoring it; if anything it will simply fester and stink."

"C'mon Monty, better days are a' comin'," Cody said. "Reagan can't be president forever."

"Alas, I will not be around to see it," Monty said, stubbing his cigarette out.

"Where'll you be?" Louis asked.

"I'll have caught the tide by then." Monty sighed and then smiled. "France, Mr. Hackenbush? Fellini is Italian. Brigitte Bardot is French." He might have said more but he was distracted by a small fire starting in the ashtray.

Louis poured water on it. "Mabel, you set the ashtray on fire," he said waving the waitress over and asking for the check and an new ashtray.

"Me?" Hackenbush put on her usual display of indignation.

"Yes, you don't stub your butts out hard enough," Louis said.

"Oh, honestly." She rolled her eyes; she was used to being accused of this. It was hardly a father-daughter event if the ashtray didn't ignite and Mabel wasn't accused of being the culprit. But all was forgiven when Louis treated her to her dinner. It was really the least he could do since he wasn't paying either her or Shorty. Ross and Cody ponied up for Shorty since they were got paid for the gig.

As usual, Hackenbush added an additional eight percent to the tip to cover the waitress tax. When Monty asked her about this and when she explained the waitress tax to him, he tossed a few more dollars on the table.

Hackenbush hugged her father good-bye; no telling when they would see each other again. The band and Monty got into the vans and headed north on the interstate. It was late and traffic was light except where CalTrans had three lanes closed for construction, which was a bore.

Dead tired, they did finally get home.

Hackenbush noticed Albany's car outside, but kept her mouth shut and hoped for the best. She wheeled a very sleepy and unusually quiet Monty into his bedroom. "I think you should take that paint off, Monty, it's bad for the skin to sleep in it," she said, fumbling for the bedside lamp switch. She squeaked in surprise when another hand brushed hers away and turned on the light. Face to face with Dr. Brazil, the most witty thing she could think of to say was, "What're you doing in there?"

"I was sleeping," Alan said thickly. "Hi, Monty."

"Hi," Monty said, perking up a little. "What are you doing in there, Alan?"

"Nathan was too tired to drive home, so he's in the guest room," Alan said matter-of-factly. "All the couches are taken. You don't mind if I sleep in here, do you, Monty?"

"Let me get this straight," Hackenbush said before Monty, who was thinking it over, could answer. "Dr. Albany is in the guestroom and you're in here?"

"Yes."

"Why?" she and Monty asked in stereo.

They got stony silence for an answer. Eventually, they got tired of that and exchanged shrugs that would have made Marcel Marceau nervous about his job. Brazil suggested that Monty come to bed, more paternally than romantically, still Hackenbush excused herself so she could blush somewhere else.

As she was washing her face, she hoped Monty had at least had the energy to take his make up off. It was the last coherent thought her exhausted brain and body could muster that night.

"Not going so well, is it, Romeo?" Hackenbush asked Nathan over coffee in the kitchen the next morning. She was having a Ramos Gin Fizz, but others were welcome to all the coffee they wanted.

"Hm... could you elaborate a little, Mabel? I haven't shaved and don't do my best thinking before I've shaved."

"I have an extra Bic razor, Nathan. Want that?" Ross offered.

"Thanks, no, I'll go home to shave," Nathan said. He finished his coffee and left.

"Why so down, Miss Mabel?" Shorty asked in an annoying falsetto.

"My efforts to drive Albany and Brazil together only seem to drive Brazil closer to Monty," she said and then explained where each member of the gay trio slept last night.

"I hope Alan and Monty were careful," Cody said.

"If you will recall, dad, Monty was dead on his feet," Hackenbush snapped. "He probably couldn't have managed even a mildly vigorous snuggle last night."

"Steady, Mabel," Ross warned. "Look on the bright side; Brazil obviously cares enough not to let Nathan drive when he's too tired."

"I don't see it that way," she said. "This is a bad development. Brazil now has fond, protective feelings for Nathan. That kind of fondness usually just cools off into platonic camaraderie and therefore all our hard work is out the window. Oh! Where did I go wrong!"

The band was thinking it over when Brazil came in and asked one of them to make Monty a Gin Fizz. Cody made it and Hackenbush delivered it to an exhausted Monty.

"You look like shit, dad," she observed blandly, handing over the drink. "I hope Alan didn't force himself on you last night."

"Tosh, Hackenbush, Alan is not that kind of man," Monty drawled softly. "He did force his opinion of you on me."

"Which is?"

"That you're the worst thing that has ever happened to him." Monty leaned back to rest for a moment. "I'm worried about this project. The whole point was to get Alan into bed with Nathan, not me."

"Yes, I feel terrible about that myself," Hackenbush agreed. "I mean, our efforts to drive him from his home and into Nathan's home aren't going very well, are they?"

Monty grunted.

"I mean, what's the worst thing we could do here that would drive Alan out of his own home?"

They thought about this and then Monty told her to get his Rolodex off the desk in the office and bring her book as well.

"What are we doing now, Violetta?" she asked, when they were seated with their address contraptions.

"Our worst, Baron Douphol; a party with every lunatic we know."

"Oooooh, you wicked wicked wicked man, you!"

"I'm a desperate desperate desperate man, Hackenbush," Monty shot back. "I want resolution and I no longer care how it's achieved."

They made lists of lists to make. They decided on a caterer and valet parking outfit. They decided to invite all the neighbors to keep the local peace. When Monty felt up to it, they moved their operations to the front room table. They dragged Shorty, Cody and Ross to the table to add names to the guest list. Envelopes came out and Monty asked them to make two for each address. When Hackenbush asked why, he said they'd use the other one for the memorial invitations.

"Oh..." she said. "How organized."

"I want you to sing, Hackenbush," Monty said, making notes on food and drink for the party and possibly for the memorial. "At both events."

"Of course, Monty. I'd be delighted."

"How's "Stardust" coming along?" he asked.

"Oh, fine. I've played through the chords once or twice," she lied.

"Shorty, please go find the Keely Smith album, I think it's called *Politely*, and put it on, thank you," Monty said.

Hackenbush liked the song, if not the bizarre rock-n-roll-ish Nelson Riddle arrangement. She thought Nelson must have seen this as a chance to cut loose or something. Keely Smith's voice didn't fare much better; Hackenbush merely allowed she had a good, solid tone, but not much nuance. It would never occur to Dr. Hackenbush that what was appropriate for the time and for the album might not be her cup of tea.

Listening to Monty's record collection did make the time pass. The selection was much improved when Ross picked out a stack to put on.

"Who's that singer?" Hackenbush asked, enchanted.

"Chet Baker."

"No!"

"Yes."

"How unfair to have so much talent in one guy," she sighed.

"And he's adorable," Monty said and asked Shorty to bring over the album to prove it: Chet Baker was cute.

While composing his invitation, Monty suggested Hackenbush ask her father, his band and all his friends to the party. This idea was met with stony silence. "What, Hackenbush?" Monty asked. "Let's not forget the purpose of this party. Is there a faster way to drive Alan out than your father and his scene?"

"Monty, you've just promoted yourself from wicked man to evil genius," Hackenbush said after a moment of worshipful awe.

"Let me get this straight," Cody said. "You're going to put the Big Daddy Hackenbush ageing hipsters in the same room with the Monty Vista theater types and expect to survive it?"

"I couldn't care less if I survive it, Cody," Monty drawled. "It's Alan I want mauled, pummeled and driven away, specifically to Nathan's place."

"Well, this will probably do it," Cody agreed.

Ross proofread the invitation and then Shorty recopied it in his best round hand. Hackenbush went off to a guy in Burbank who seemed never to sleep and had half a dozen copy machines in his living room. The original plan had been to hand write each invitation, but their arms were falling off just from addressing envelopes so they decided to dispense with the niceties. As long as there was food, drink and wild abandon, their friends would understand photocopied invitations. While waiting for the copies, she invited the guy because she'd known him for years and he was very understanding of all the slightly hysterical, completely exhausted musicians who came in for copies on their way to the gig or the studio session or in the middle of the night. He said he could not leave his house; what if someone needed copies that night? Hackenbush could certainly understand that.

On her way back she considered dropping by her apartment, but she didn't feel up to seeing the phone machine. She picked up a pizza at Sam's Pizza and went back to Chez Monty, where she spent the rest of the afternoon stuffing envelopes and singing variations on "Stardust" with the band. They scrounged up enough stamps and Cody, who had his own errands to run anyway, took them to the post office while Hackenbush and Shorty delivered the invitations to the neighbors. The neighbors said they would be delighted to attend; Hackenbush dearly hoped so.

Over the next few days, RSVPs poured in right and left. A few invitations came back with expired forwarding addresses but most of those address-unknown guests were mercilessly tracked down and invited. It was shaping to be a wonderful brawl; at least the caterers were delighted.

In the process of catering negotiations, the caterer hired Dr. Hackenbush and her Orchestra to do a fill-in at a Westside evening wedding reception. Of course they accepted; gigs like this paid hugely and they even negotiated a bonus out of the caterer for the short notice. No one had to know Hackenbush, Ross and Cody had nothing better to do that Thursday night and luckily Phil Noyes was able to send a sub to a previous commitment.

Although she'd survived the bowling alley, Hackenbush still felt ambivalent about singing. She was looking forward to getting dressed up and making some money, but the spark of excitement still hadn't come back to her. Maybe it never would and that was something she'd have to face fairly soon. Life hardly seemed worth living without Eddy Lee, but was life worth living at all without Eddy and music? It was way too much to think about on a weekday; she might tackle it over the weekend.

Hackenbush had a long, slinky black evening gown she wore for formal casuals. Monty had garment bags full of evening gowns left over from various productions and an unfortunate drag experiment in the 1970s. He turned his nose up at her description of her dress and sent her upstairs with very specific instructions on what to bring down.

The dress was a thick matte black silk, heavily trimmed with rhinestones at the bottom so it looked like Hackenbush was standing on a pedestal of stars. Or pedestal of rhinestones, for the literalist crowd. The rhinestones swirled up and thinned out at her waist, where jet sequins took over, scattering artistically over the bodice. It weighed a ton and had a corset-like assembly that laced up in back to support the weight of the dress and the curves of the wearer. She had complained to Monty (it was his dress, after all) that she didn't know how she was supposed to sing when she could hardly breathe.

"Are these wedding guests expecting the jazz Maria Callas?" he asked.

"No."

"Then who cares how you sound, my dear. It's all in how you look."

Well, that was true. The draperies fastened in back and Shorty had spent the early part of his evening sewing her into it and it now fit like a glove. Corset contraption notwithstanding, one good rip and the whole mess would be in a sparkly pool at her feet. But some risks are worth taking, and this was one of them; she looked gorgeous.

Even Dr. Albany gave her an appreciative whistle when he came in. Of course this whistle included Cody and Ross, magnificent in their tuxedoes.

"You are going to be here to cut me free later, right, Shorty?" she asked over her bare shoulder.

"I wouldn't miss it for the world," he said and wished them a good night. It was a strictly music gig, so he was staying home to play board games with the docs and Monty. Hackenbush had called it a positively domestic evening and suggested they add charades to the schedule. Monty told her if she hadn't asphyxiated by the time she got home, they might try a few with her. But Monty had been in bed for hours by the time she got home.

Saturday was on the busy side. Hackenbush saw no point in tidying the joint up since the hordes were descending in less than twelve hours, but Shorty and Cody insisted they give it the once over. Lucky Ross was substitute teaching at the Grove School of Music that afternoon so he escaped the cleaning frenzy, which only lasted for an hour.

Alan had protested this party nonstop since he'd seen the first RSVP come in. He was soundly ignored by everyone except Nathan who listened sympathetically, while hoping the alterations on his new tuxedo would be ready by Saturday. He'd bought it the day he'd gotten his invitation to the party. So, yes indeed, he was listening sympathetically, even tenderly, to Alan's complaints, but he was definitely in the pro-party camp. In fact, the only people in the anti-party camp were Alan and the curmudgeon neighbor over the back fence. But even he changed sides when Hackenbush put on a tight skirt and went over and reasoned with him.

So, realizing he was facing a complete rout, Alan barricaded himself in his bedroom with books and journals to occupy him while his house was invaded. He was surprised to find his tuxedo, which hadn't seen any action in that decade and most of the one before it, aired, pressed and hanging accusingly on his closet door. He put it back in the closet where he wouldn't see it.

Hackenbush figured correctly that she'd end up being

the surrogate hostess and so put on a smart black dress and her trusty pumps, the best shoes for running around at your own party in. She directed the caterers to set up the buffet and barbeque in the back yard and gave the valet parking crew an early dinner and lots of snacks and drinks to sustain them through the evening. She was pleased to see all the valets had skateboards to zip around on; good idea, since it would be street parking and could be blocks away. The postcards for Dr. Hackenbush and her Orchestra's October concert had been printed and she placed them in strategic places around the house. And, lastly, she decided to dump the coats and bags in the guest bedroom upstairs; after all, Brazil would be at the party and not need his bedroom.

Ross was busy setting up a borrowed student drum kit so other players could sit in and he wouldn't have to worry about his own skins. It was not the greatest set of drums in the world, but they would do for the purposes of this particular evening. The other cats would bring their own stuff and by the apex of the evening, Dr. Brazil's office was bursting with instrument cases. Phil showed up early and while Hackenbush ran around organizing stuff, the rhythm section got the right mood going.

When the first guests arrived at eight-thirty, Monty emerged in a basic black tuxedo and looking very lovely. He'd spent the day in bed to conserve his energy for the party, probably his last one. But one would never know it by the suave greetings he slathered on everyone from his armchair.

Piled high with coats and bags, Hackenbush staggered upstairs and barged into Alan's lair. "Hi, what are you doing in here?" she asked, dumping the coats on the end of the bed.

"It's my room; get out," Alan snarled. "And take those with you." He waved vaguely at the coats and bags.

"Come down for the party," she said. "We had your tux pressed and we're putting the coats in here."

"I'm not coming to the party and..." He was distracted by the entrance of a coat-laden Shorty. "And you can put the coats in my office downstairs."

"That's where we're putting the instrument cases," Shorty said on his way out.

"Hey, d'you think this is a mink?" Hackenbush asked,

stroking a fur coat.

"I wouldn't know," Alan said, kicking a few coats off his bed.

"Well, I'll hang it in here anyway," she said, opening the closet. She pulled out Alan's tuxedo while she was at it. "Look, I bet you look cute in this, Dr. Brazil. Why not put it on and come downstairs?" she asked in her best guy-coaxing voice.

"No."

Hackenbush tossed a few coats from the floor onto the bed and left. She passed Shorty in the hall. "He's not in a pretty mood," she warned.

"Neither is Monty," Shorty said. "He needs, and badly needs, you downstairs."

Hackenbush made tracks and found Monty surrounded by old friends. She collected coats while being introduced and smiled politely at men wearing more and better applied eye make-up than she. Most impressive.

"Where's darling Alan!?" one of the painted guys asked.

"Yeah, where is Dr. Dreamboat?" another heavily rouged guy asked.

"Upstairs..." Monty drawled, looking a question at Hackenbush. "Dressing?"

"Sulking," she said.

"Well, we can't have that," a new comer said.

"Carlysis! How the devil are you?" Monty roared. "Hackenbush! This is Carlysis!"

"How-de-do?" she said, taking his coat. This Carlysis was just the way Hackenbush liked them: tall, dark and handsome and, as usual, queer as a three-dollar bill. He was, however, un-painted and lightly scented and gave her a stagy wink she quite thoroughly approved of.

While this conversation was in progress, tall, blonde and handsome Lola Rae, recently returned from her stint dancing in the Bay Area, had wandered upstairs looking for a peaceful mirror to refresh her make-up. She barged in on Alan, who was telling Shorty in no uncertain terms to take the fucking coats out of his bedroom or he'd start throwing them on the lawn.

"That would show the proper spirit, darling man, but the

valet parking guys are all over the lawn already," Lola drawled. "And they need that lawn. Bye-bye, Shorty," she said waving him out of the room. She seated herself on the edge of Alan's bed and crossed her long, powerful dancer's legs. She was five foot ten and wearing an astonishingly skimpy evening gown, so it was quite a show. "Shall I call you Cinderella? Has no one invited you to the ball?" she cooed.

"They have and I won't go."

"No?!"

"No."

"Whyzat, cutie-pie? Looks like it's gonna be a real nice brawl," she said, bored with being posh and happily back to her more natural speech. She glanced up at Shorty delivering another load of coats. There were now no un-coated surfaces in there. She frowned him out of the room. "Why won't you go to the party? Although I just met him, Monty Vista seems like a helluva nice guy."

"Yes, I know. It's Hackenbush I hate," Alan said, pouting a little.

"Reeeeaaaaallllly?" Lola liked Hackenbush a little but liked to torment her a lot and any excuse would do. "What's she done?"

"She's throwing this party when I asked her not to."

"I thought it was Mr. Vista's party?"

"Well, yes, but, um..."

"You poor thing," Lola soothed. "Never mind, it probably is all Hackenbush's fault, even if it's not. I know! Would you like me to beat her up for you?"

A man of peace, a healer, a scientist and a scholar— Alan Brazil, M.D., thought this over for a full five seconds and said, "Yes."

"Then come watch! It's no fun without an audience!" Lola led him downstairs, but stopped at the entrance to the big room. "Can you see from here?" she asked and he nodded. "Keep those beautiful eyes peeled. And when I'm done with her, you go right up and get dressed up and come back down and dance with me. That's my reward." She swaggered across the floor to where Hackenbush, relieved of her coat burden by Shorty, was introducing a guitar player named Joey

Bell (who was waiting for Phil to take a break so he could play) to the tall, dark and handsome Carlysis.

"Oh, hi Lola, this is–" Hackenbush edged away, but not quickly enough.

Wham! Lola's roundhouse slap knocked the singer's glasses flying.

"Ow! Lola! What the fuck?!"

Lola would have let fly again except Joey grabbed her wrists and walked her back a few steps.

"Lola, Lola, Lola! I say, I say, Lola honey it's too early in the evening to beat up Hackenbush yet," Joey said, doing his Foghorn Leghorn impersonation. "Look at me when I'm talkin' to you, gal."

"Oooooh..." Lola batted her big blue eyes at him. "So there IS something to look forward to! Let's dance, Joey."

Joey didn't mind, and it was probably the most peaceful way to get Lola away from Hackenbush at that moment.

"Friend of yours, Miss Hackenbush?" Carlysis asked, handing her her glasses that he'd so thoughtfully retrieved.

"Well, not really," she admitted. "But now that she's back, it's not a party without Lola Rae. Oh! Or Suzy Reed! There she is!" Hackenbush pointed to another tall, powerful, but brunette, dancer dumping her coat on Shorty. "I'll show you to Alan, now," she added. They followed Shorty upstairs and found Alan's room empty but for waist-high drifts of coats. "Where the hell is he?" she asked Shorty.

"Beats me, maybe he made a break for it," Shorty said, leaving the room.

Hackenbush started to say, "Well, shi–", when Alan's closet door opened and he came out resplendent in his tuxedo.

"Carlysis! How nice to see you!" Alan's mood was much improved by Lola smacking Hackenbush. He even smiled at the victim.

"Alan! Nice to see you, too. And just out of the closet—how delightful!" The two men left the room arm in arm.

Hackenbush sighed, rubbed her stinging cheek and hung up a few more fur coats. Since she couldn't tell a fox from a sable, she failed to be suitably impressed, but did know which coats to hang up and which to let lie. She did, however, think it was too hot for furs, but fur-owning women in Los Angeles don't let the weather get in the way of fashion. Ever.

When she got back downstairs, she found Alan standing next to Monty, very cordially greeting guests. She gave Lola, now dancing with Suzy, a wide berth and went outside to see if the valet parking guys needed anything. They were fine and as they zipped around in cars or on skateboards, looked like they were having fun, too.

She was about to go inside when Big Daddy Hackenbush arrived. He tossed the keys to his American-made wreck of a car to a valet and told the kid not to scratch the paint. He looked pleased to see his only acknowledged child standing before him.

"Hi, daddy, are you stag tonight?" she asked, turning her cheek up for a fatherly kiss.

"Yes," Louis said, "Darla decided not to come because you weren't very friendly at the bowling alley."

"Who's Darla?" Hackenbush asked.

"Never mind, Mabel." He put his arm around her and they went inside where there was a whole lot of saxophone soloing going on. Possibly too much.

Louis put his horn together while saying hello to Monty. "You'll be a welcome addition, Mr. Hackenbush," Monty drawled over the cascading flood of notes.

"I guess so," Louis said. "Mabel, why the hell did you invite so many sax players?"

"I was told to collect all the lunatics I could find," she said simply. She might have said more but Louis and Monty were laughing too hard so she took Louis's clarinet case into Alan's office. She noticed the silly man hadn't put any identification on the case, so she took one of her own cards and put it inside.

Even with some of the mob eating in the backyard and some smoking in the front yard or strolling in the street, the room was jammed. People were not only dancing cheek-to-cheek, they were standing cheek-to-cheek. "Any more invited guests and we'll need a shoe-horn and some Crisco," she thought. "Well, here's one more and very necessary." Through a certain amount of brute strength and force of personality, Hackenbush managed to wedge Nathan through the crowd and into Monty's presence.

"Nathan! It's too wonderful! Where's Alan!" Monty had a few and was in full cry by then. "Alan! Alan!"

Alan politely excused himself from where he was politely listening to Aunt Marie yelling the details of her gallbladder operation into his ear. "Hello, Nathan, glad you could make it," Alan said pleasantly at the top of his voice.

"Yes, um... thanks," Nathan shouted back. He glanced at the people around him, they all seemed to be watching him and Alan with an intense and unnerving interest, especially Monty and Hackenbush.

"Um, let's get you a drink," Alan suggested. He'd noticed the strange scrutiny, too. He led Nathan away to the bar in the backyard.

"Monty, are you sure those two are in love?" one of the guys near him asked when the docs had gone.

"Of course!" Monty rolled his eyes at Hackenbush.

She laughed and excused herself to greet Anna Kodaly. "Hi, Anna!" she screamed, just to be heard.

The temp employment specialist nearly jumped out of her skin. "Oh, Mabel! God, you scared the hell out of me," she said.

"What?"

"You scared the hell out of me!" Anna yelled back. "Thanks for inviting me!"

"You're welcome! Drinks and grub in the backyard; dancing and screaming in here! I'll take your coat!"

"Thanks! Can you introduce me to the host?" Anna yelled.

"Yes! This way!" Hackenbush led her over to Monty. "Monty, this is Anna Kodaly, she who booked me to work at Alan's lab that fateful day."

"Really? Miss Kodaly, I salute you," Monty roared. "Hackenbush has been a lifesaver, a comfort, a balm, and an excellent secretary, taking down my memoirs as if they were her own."

"She's working as a secretary for you?" Anna asked, triple forte.

"Yes! And beautifully, too!"

"Anna, it's not what you think..." Hackenbush began.

"We'll talk later, Mabel," Anna yelled and headed for the backyard.

Hackenbush milled around, picking up empty glasses, putting out abandoned cigarettes and yelling greetings to newcomers. She took coats upstairs, where she further buried Alan's bed. An intrepid couple was making good use of Alan's bed nevertheless. She took this as a sign that the party was in high gear because there was also an orgy in progress in Monty's bedroom. She'd considered breaking it up, but figured she'd just be torn to pieces for no reason. Amazingly, when the police did show up, they were very good natured about it; they only asked the valet guys not to park any more cars on the sidewalk and went away with some sandwiches Hackenbush had the caterers make for them. "Tell the next shift to drop by for supper if they feel like it," she said as they were leaving. "I'm sure we'll still be here."

Back inside, she found Anna in her coat, saying good night to Monty. "Leaving so early, Anna?" Hackenbush asked, handing her an October concert postcard and walking her outside.

"This is late for me, Mabel," Anna said as she dug out her key ticket for the valet guy. "I lead a very quiet, sheltered life, but not for much longer."

"Oh?"

"Yeah, I'm opening my own agency in a few weeks," Anna said, watching for her car. "Can I call you to work for me?"

"Absolutely! You better or my feelings will be very hurt," Hackenbush said. "What brought this on?"

"Well, to sit is to stagnate and to stagnate is to die, right?" Anna handed the valet a buck and tossed her bag on the front seat.

"I couldn't agree more," Hackenbush said. Anna was her favorite temp booker and she hoped she had what it took to run her own business. Entrepreneurial fervor had managed to elude Hackenbush all her life. She thought small business owners were nuts, but, oh well; what did she know? "Temporary Solutionations won't like the competition much."

"Oh, they can go to hell," Anna said and drove away into the night.

"Wow, how entrepreneurial," Hackenbush said and went back into the house. She found Nathan crammed into a corner by himself. "Oh, hello, want to dance?" she asked and he did, quite nicely, too.

By this time, word of the Alan and Nathan romance had spread to every corner of the room. However, the big question was, "If they're so in love, why aren't they spending more time together?" This was bothering Lola Rae enough that she cornered Shorty and terrorized the whole, weird story out of him. "Oh! Leave it to Hackenbush to fuck up a perfectly straightforward situation!" she cried, shaking her fists over his head.

The furious Lola went back in the house and her rage impossibly notched up when she saw Hackenbush innocently dancing with Nathan. Looking around, she found Alan talking to a group of guys and she stalked over. "Ah ha! My reward!" she screamed and grabbed his arm. "I'll lead," she said, dancing away with the stunned man.

Lola was a very strong woman and even stronger when she was a woman with a mission. Not only did she propel Alan through the dancing throng; the force of impact when she slammed him into Hackenbush and Nathan nearly shook their fillings loose. "Oh, excuse me," she said, a more demented than usual light in her eyes. "Change partners!" And she dragged Hackenbush away.

Because they were crushed together and there was no easy way to leave the dance floor, or perhaps they were afraid of what Lola would do if they didn't dance, or maybe even because it seemed like a good idea, Nathan took Alan in his arms and danced with him.

"Please don't hurt me, Lola!" Hackenbush wailed as Lola pushed her toward the band.

"Maybe later, Hackenbush," Lola yelled at her. "But isn't it time for little runts like you to sing, Goddamn it?" Lola smiled terrifyingly as she maneuvered Hackenbush in front of the microphone.

"Oh," Hackenbush said, putting the mike stand between herself and the dancer, who melted back into the crowd.

"Hackenbush! Hackenbush!" Monty yelled. "Sing "Stardust"!"

"Oh, okay." Hackenbush was tired as she listened to the four bar intro. She looked around the room and her eyes fell on Alan and Nathan, dancing happily, and she felt like there might be hope for love there. For her, there would never be love or even hope for it again. She would have the memory to torment her.

She sang the verse. It really was a beautiful song. Maybe she would just have beautiful songs in her life. Songs about the sadness of lost love, hope for new love and always longing for what she didn't have.

She would never love anyone again like she loved Eddy Lee; it was a love that happens once. And, in truth, she knew most people never experienced that kind of love ever. It was rare, it was incredible and even if she didn't measure everything against it...

She could get the fuck on with her life and sing her heart out again. She filled her lungs with the first refreshing full breath she'd drawn since Eddy left her. And sang.

Something like joy coursed through the room. Not joy exactly, but there is no word for when the singer is so free in her song, in the moment, that she transports her listeners beyond their fears and concerns and into a purity of feeling that, well, is called joy, for want of a better word.

Monty looked on and was glad he got to hear this before he died.

Nathan held Alan a little closer.

Lola Rae grabbed Shorty and shook him and then made him dance with her. And Shorty didn't care; he was thanking all the deities he could think of for Hackenbush's miraculous recovery. He caught Ross' and then Cody's eye and knew they were thanking the same gods he was.

And Hackenbush just let the song sing through her, something that had not happened in far too long. Whatever unlucky spirit that protects singers must have heaved a huge sigh of relief and gone off to work on someone else's problems because Hackenbush's were solved.

Even the best of friends have got to part one day and even the wildest parties wind down and die. Monty's went on until the wee small hours; the caterers were long gone, the valets brought the last few cars up, handed back the keys, took their skateboards and tips and went home for a well-earned rest. Since nobody volunteered to make breakfast, the last few lingering guests said good-bye, wasn't this fun?, we must do this again someday, I'll call you, and finally toddled off. This left Hackenbush, Ross, Cody, Monty, Shorty, Alan and Nathan, who was pretty much a member of the family by then, sitting happy and exhausted in the post-party wreckage. They were discussing various guests and Hackenbush commented that Carlysis was quite handsome.

"Not your type, Mabel," Shorty told her.

"Yeah, I noticed," she sighed, tired but too happy to notice.

"Carlysis is looking well, don't you think Alan?" Monty said. "About how I was looking a year ago."

Alan merely nodded.

"He tells me I'm missed at the baths," Monty continued. "He said these past few months have been quite dull without me."

Hackenbush looked puzzled. "Few months?" she asked. "You were at the bathhouse a few months ago?"

"Dear me, look at the time, I–" Alan began.

"Of course, Hackenbush," Monty drawled. "I was famous in the baths, to paraphrase Dylan."

"Having sex?" she asked bluntly.

"Why else go to the baths?"

"Safe sex?"

"Heavens no; what a bore, what a waste of time,"

"You mean you didn't stop having sex when you knew you had AIDS?" Hackenbush asked.

"Well, of course not, Hackenbush," Monty drawled. "When I still had the strength for the chase I was still at it. How else would it be?"

"And did you tell these guys you were having unsafe sex with that you had AIDS?" she asked.

Sensing danger, Monty did not answer her.

"I thought not," she said softly. The table went very still and Hackenbush just stared at him. She was too tired of the situation to be nice; she would save Alan from Monty and Monty's ghost, as she had been saved from Eddy Lee's ghost tonight. It would be ugly, but, based on this new information she had about Monty, it would be necessary. 'Girls get all the dirty jobs, don't we? Like smacking sense into guys what ought to know better. Oh well,' she thought bitterly. Something went out behind her eyes and she turned to look at Alan.

"So, Dr. Brazil," she said quietly. "Here you are, this big deal doctor, trying to solve the mystery of cancer, AIDS, what have you and all your patients die."

"Hackenbush!" Nathan hissed at her.

"It's all right," Alan said, laying his hand on Nathan's. "All my patients do die; that's how it is with fatal diseases. I do my best, but people die of them eventually."

"And that's your best? Wouldn't your best, your very best be to make it so they didn't get these diseases?" she asked mildly.

"I can't do anything about most cancers—"

"I'm not talking about cancer; I'm talking about AIDS," she cut him off. "You live with a guy who knew what he had and still was spreading the most horrible disease I can remember in my lifetime. Horrible, insidious and incurable."

"Jesus, Mabel." Cody leaned away from the table and looked ill. No one seemed to notice.

"At the time, we didn't know exactly how the virus was transmitted—"

"Horse shit, Dr. Brazil, everybody knew or strongly suspected that if you took it up the ass, you got AIDS," she said coolly. "Even we stupid women got to know that right from the start."

"Speculation..." Alan began.

"...was all we had on AIDS for quite a while, if you will recall." She leaned back and lit a cigarette. "But my point is, how do you, Dr. Brazil, reconcile your loyalty to Monty—charming, sexy, infectious, fatal Monty—with your commitment to healing?"

"My personal life—"

"You have seen lots of people die of AIDS, Alan," she snapped. "How can you face yourself knowing you live with and support someone who has, is and will be responsible for who knows how many deaths because all he cares about is his dick? Have you been surrounded by death for so long, you can't stop it when it's right in front of you?"

White with fury, Alan leaned across the table and snarled, "What was I supposed to do, Hackenbush?"

"We can't do anything about the past, can we, Dr. Brazil? But in the present, we have before us a unique opportunity to let the selfish, fatal bastard redeem himself." She gestured graciously at Monty. "Although he does not care for the health and welfare of others, he has enough human feeling left for you to want to see you happy before he dies. In fact, to make sure you're happy before he dies. So the least you can do is run off with Dr. Albany so we can all get some sleep tonight."

"That would be disloyal, Hackenbush," Brazil said, leaning back.

"Loyalty is beautiful up to the point of diminishing returns, Dr. Brazil," she sighed. "Monty might have been worthy of your loyalty once, in those days before he started spreading this horrendous disease, but now? Why ever would you be loyal to the Typhoid Mary of AIDS? Why, when all is said and done, I bet Monty's killed more people than the serial killer we got running around the Southland right now."

"Mabel!" Shorty gasped, scandalized. Like Cody, he leaned away from the table.

"But wicked, old, evil, diseased, infectious, dying Monty wants to do one right thing before he goes, maybe the only right thing he's ever done in his whole selfish, sex ridden existence, and that's to finally shake you off and into a better life," Hackenbush continued. "This is not the time to get stubborn, Alan, when you should be going home with Nathan."

"I don't see how this is any of your business, Hackenbush," Alan said dismissively.

"I don't see how you want to watch Monty die and be alone with the fact that, yes, he's dead but many many others will die horribly because of him," she said. "I don't see how you can turn away a decent chance to love and be happy out of some twisted sense of loyalty to Monty, who's never really given much of a damn about you until he realized that saving you from living in a post-Vista hell might save him from Hell itself. I don't see how denying Monty this one last and final thing he wants from you will make up for all the years where you denied him nothing. I don't see how breaking Nathan's and Monty's hearts by being stubbornly set on fag martyrdom is going to do anyone the slightest bit of good. It's not like anyone is going to write an opera about how big and brave you were, Alan. Likely you'll just fade away or end up like the Moodys of the world in that hellish netherworld seclusion where suicide and actual living are much the same and also too much work; so you won't bother, you'll just rot. But you like rot, Dr. Brazil; you'll sit and rot and regret that you didn't do the one thing that would have kept Monty from haunting you for the rest of your fucking life. This is your big chance to escape all that, Alan. Or have you been surrounded by death for so long, you crave it now and can't see a way out of it when it's right in front of you?"

Nobody said anything or screamed or lunged across the table or sneezed or anything of any sort while Alan Brazil, M.D., stared into Mabel Hackenbush, vocalist's, eyes. Nothing changed in his face when he turned his head and said to Nathan, "Please take me out of here," and mere seconds passed before the door closed behind them and they were gone.

There was a moment of silence except for the sound of all the tension whooshing out of the room and the musicians inhaling. Like the rest of them, Monty had been frozen but came out of it slowly with them and said, "Mabel, you cunt."

"Monty, from a guy like you, that's a compliment," she sighed, lighting a cigarette and picking a shred of tobacco off her tongue.

"I will not be judged by a gash like you," he continued.

"Too late! I have judged you and what fucking difference does it make? None." She stood up and began to gather her things and shove them into her shoulder bag. "Because, in the end, I have finally, though tenuously, accomplished what you asked: I've driven Alan into Nathan's arms and I am damn glad of it! I can't save you, Monty, nothing can save you. I can't even like you anymore. I thought we were the same: weary, jaded, bored, blasé, and pained by the cruel and ugly world we must live in. But,

Monty, much as I might have hated life in the recent past, much as my heart is pretty much still broken and life feels like a burden because it sometimes is, I would never deliberately add to the cruelty and ugliness of the world by infecting anyone with AIDS when I knew I had it, no matter what."

"There you are judging me again."

"Of course, it's a judgment call to have sex when you know you're carrying the virus," she said. "It's bad judgment by a bad man."

"Fuck you, Hackenbush," Monty snarled. "You just have to accept me the way I am."

"Monty, I have to accept the fact that you are the way you are," she said, picking up her briefcase. "I don't have to have anything to do with you." She waved at the band and left.

A few moments of silence went by before Shorty said he thought he'd do the dishes. Ross and Cody began collecting plates and glasses from all over the room. No one really noticed when Monty went to bed; he seemed to want to be alone, so that's how they left him.

Alan hardly noticed the drive the Nathan's place, he was too busy staring into the horrible past and the uncharted future. He hated both. He'd become a doctor to avoid the vague and nagging questions of life, such as what was right and what was wrong and having a creature like Hackenbush point those out to him was just injury onto insult.

He loved Monty, or thought he did. Now he wondered if he just loved the idea of loving Monty and all the suffering that went with it. 'What do I know about love?' he asked himself, and then felt sorry for Nathan.

Oh. Nathan. Alan recalled with a start that he was in Nathan's car, going to Nathan's place, presumably to Nathan's bed. Oh dear. Oh well. He'd come this far, or rather, he'd been shoved this far by Hackenbush; he thought he'd not let Nathan (and Monty in some way) down. One of Alan's problems with life was that he was never sure if he was resigned, committed or engaged with it. This was not something he was likely to work out between northeast LA and upper Glendale that night, so he just relaxed and watched the freeway go by.

Dr. Albany, on the other hand, was very nervous. He was on the verge of getting what he'd thought was impossible and he had a bad case of the jitters. Right up to the very last moment when Alan had asked him to take him away from there, Nathan thought it was a lost cause. He thought Hackenbush's terrifying recital would simply drive Alan closer to Monty. He'd been shocked that it had jolted his hopefully soon-to-be lover loose from Monty. Still he was nervous leading Alan into his apartment. "Um, I could sleep on the couch," he offered.

"No, I... would you like me to sleep on the couch, Nathan?" Alan asked.

"No... no, not at all."

They stared at their feet for a few moments before Alan asked, "Could I take a shower?"

"Of course!" Nathan showed him the bathroom off his bedroom. When the door was firmly closed, Nathan changed into his pajamas and turned off the bedside lamp. He was nervous. He didn't have much sexual experience and that was mostly some clumsy, but earnest, fumbling around in the various backseats of his youth. He hoped Alan wouldn't be offended or annoyed by his lack of finesse and that his sincerity and eagerness to please would be enough. He could only hope, he could only try, he could only... He could only watch Alan come out of the bathroom and toss the towel around his waist to the end of the bed. He could only wait for what happened next and hope for the best. It was too late to worry anymore, too late for fear or regret; there was only hope, wonder and a quick prayer for the best possible fulfillment of all his dreams.

And when Alan Brazil slipped into his bed and into his arms so perfectly, as he should and always would, what else was there to say or want or wonder about?

Hackenbush just went home without dreading it for the first time in so long she'd lost track. She got home and cleared her messages. She took the cassette out and held it in her hand. It still had Eddy Lee's last words to her carefully preserved in magnetic media on it. She thought she'd run out the door and

Ginger Mayerson

down to the lake where she'd fling it into the depths and declare whatever a woman declares in a moment like that. But it was 4 AM and only a suicidal crazy woman would go anywhere on foot at that hour in Echo Park if she didn't have to. Hackenbush lit a cigarette and turned the tape in her hands. It was a newish tape, still had lots of tread on it, seemed a shame to waste it by burning it or throwing it in the lake or whatever. So, thrifty to her well worn heels, she put it back in the machine and erased it—all of it—and went to bed.

The rest she heard from Cody and Shorty over the next few months. Cody very kindly collected whatever she'd left at Monty's and brought it over the following afternoon. As she had suspected, the moment Alan and Nathan got together, Monty began to try to undermine their romance. Not that Cody and Shorty, or Ross for that matter, could do anything about it except exchange shrugs with Alan. But the shrugging seemed to help. If Monty's behavior bothered Nathan, well, he kept it to himself.

Ross moved into his own place a few weeks later. He thanked Monty and Alan for helping him out during his homeless period and left. This had startled Alan, who later asked Shorty about it.

"Yes," Shorty had said. "Except for Mabel, we all lost our places to live about the time she and Monty started this project. Did you think we were all here just to torment you?"

"Well, I..."

"We really did want to see you and Nathan get together," Shorty said. "Nathan likes you a lot and we like him."

"What about me?" Alan asked.

"Oh, we know you like Nathan."

If Shorty felt lonely at Casa Vista when Cody moved up to Altadena, he never let on. He didn't really have time for loneliness because Monty took a turn for the worse and was hospitalized for a while. When Monty came home, Shorty, Alan, Nathan and the visiting nurses were very busy looking after him. Alan became very depressed and though he hid it from Monty and the nurses, he leaned heavily on Nathan and even a little on Shorty.

Ross moved Shorty to his place to get some rest before the show in October. He and Cody and Cody's new girlfriend, whom everyone agreed was the catch of the century, took turns helping out at Monty's. They marveled at Brazil and Albany; even if those two were trained in medicine and devoted their lives to helping people, their strength and compassion were still amazing.

"When I die I hope somebody takes care of me like this," Ross had grumbled to Nathan one evening on his way out.

"Just don't die this week, Ross," Nathan said, giving his shoulder a warm squeeze. "I have tickets to your show."

"Hm. Are you bringing Alan?" Ross asked.

"No... no, Alan is still annoyed at Hackenbush." He held up a hand to forestall whatever Ross was going to say. "I know, it's not logical or even really nice, but these are not logical or nice times, are they? I'm bringing my sister; she'll love it."

Nathan's sister turned up at Monty's a few times to make meals and clean the place. She was a nice lady in her early forties who listened to Dr. Toni Grant while she cleaned and cooked. She must have known what a great guy her brother was, but even she was impressed by the way he took care of Monty (and Alan, for that matter). She liked Alan very much, and in her own quiet way seemed to be welcoming him into the family.

And she did enjoy the show very much. Everyone enjoyed the show very much, except the LA Times, which didn't seem to hear about it. The Weekly and the Reader gave it raves. "Hackenbush is back!" one story began, which caused Mabel to realize how long she'd been mourning Eddy Lee.

In spite of this triumph and the series of gigs that came along, including a few that were longer than two weeks, she still had bad moments. She kept busy, she found a house that needed to be saved in Lincoln Heights, cut a killer five-year rent deal, and moved there after spending a month breaking her and all her friends' backs fixing it up. It was a beaut though: hardwood floors, moulded ceilings, deco fixtures, a big bathtub in an alcove, and a balcony facing west with a panoramic view over the 5 freeway from Griffith Park, the backside of downtown and all the way down to County Hospital. It was better than television, it had to be because Hackenbush's reception went to hell there and she was too cheap to pay for cable. The house was built on a hill, so the first floor was only a half floor and used for storage (mostly by her friends) and she lived on the second floor. It was the coolest house she'd ever lived in, but even that couldn't quite get her over Eddy Lee.

She heard from Shorty that Monty got well enough to take complete credit for the success of their show. Hackenbush merely rolled her eyes. Shorty told her that Nathan moved in when Shorty found a place to live. Of the four of them, Shorty was the only one who kept in contact after the show. Monty got better; Monty got worse; Monty got better; Monty got worse. Hackenbush finally asked not to be updated; she couldn't care less what happened to Monty fucking Vista.

So she didn't hear about him. She gigged with the band, worked out new dance routines with Shorty, had a huge Christmas Day party to show off her new place and so she wouldn't have to be alone that day. Eddy fucking Lee had been very big on Christmas and the few she'd had with him were the best she could remember.

"Oh, fuck the past, fuck all of it!" She found herself saying a lot in January, a quiet month for gigs. She worked for Anna's new agency, Temporary Insanity, and was glad to see it succeed. Anna was as cool as an agency owner as she was as a lowly temp booker. If all of capitalism could be like Anna then utopia could only be just around the corner.

One night when she couldn't sleep, she got up and lit a cigarette. It was cold outside but she needed air and stepped onto the balcony to watch her sleeping neighborhood. It was too late to play records or call anybody and she was bored by her books. She couldn't shake her blues. She tried to let them spin out but they just coiled a little tighter in her chest. "Ah, y'bastards; are you going to make life more of a burden than it's really worth?" she wondered. A few cars went by below. That was not unusual, even at that hour, what was unusual was the dun colored sedan with no lights on that pulled up beside her balcony...her second floor balcony.

The raggedy guy she'd given a cigarette in front of Monty's many months ago rolled down the window. He was smoking, possibly it was the same cigarette. "Ride, lady?"

Hackenbush blinked a few times and wondered what Phillip Morris was putting in Pall Malls these days. She thought she saw someone in the back seat, but couldn't make out who it was. She blinked a few more times and since the hallucination was not going to go away, she figured she better answer. "Uh, no thanks, I have to work tomorrow."

"Later then, doc," he said, rolling up the window and pulling away. He turned on the brightest headlights Hackenbush had ever seen, except once before, as she watched him drive out of sight.

"Oh, great. Big lights to wake up the neighborhood," she thought. But the night was as quiet as it was and the cars that went by below had normal headlights. Hackenbush finished her cigarette and tried to decide if she'd missed an opportunity or just had a narrow escape or was merely dreaming. In which case, she hoped she wasn't burning her house down by smoking in her sleep.

In the afternoon, Ross left a message on her machine that Shorty had called him to say Monty died last night and that he, Ross, wanted to see her after work at the Onyx.

She was a little late due to traffic, but Ross was there, waiting patiently. "Well?" she asked wedging herself into the corner table of the tiny café.

"Shorty and Cody said he had one last request, that we–"

"Monty had plenty of requests and I'm done doing his bidding," she snapped and ordered a café au lait.

Ross let her drink a little before he began again. "That we, including you, sing at his memorial. He wants you to sing "Stardust" again, the way you sang it at–"

"Fuck, Ross," she hissed furiously. "The guy was fucking around when he knew–"

"Mabel. It's a very fucked up world, seems like a strange place to hold a grudge against a dead guy."

Ross wrote down the when and where and left it on the table for her. She thought it was a little late in the evening to have a memorial, but Monty had been a night owl anyway.

Ginger Mayerson

***

Alan thought he was emotionally prepared for Monty's death. He was wrong; he fell apart and when he wasn't thanking God for Nathan, Shorty and Nathan's sister for being there for him; he was resenting the hell out of them.

He wondered why he deserved their help and compassion when he was such a rotten person that he couldn't even keep Monty home and safe. He felt unworthy because he'd fallen in love with Nathan while Monty was still alive, even though that was what Monty wanted, but still. Well, it was all Hackenbush's fault anyway. Or something. He couldn't really think about it now. He tried to take a few days off, but being around the house was too horrible. He was stunned and numb and didn't really even notice that Shorty and Nathan were stuffing envelopes and making arrangements on the phone. He kept hearing the word 'memorial' and slowly realized...

"Are you organizing a memorial for Monty?" he asked them one night at dinner.

"No, we're just following the instructions he left," Nathan said.

"Instructions?"

"Yeah, that's one of the things he did with Mabel," Shorty said, consulting his neatly typed list. "They worked out where to hold the memorial, who to invite, what to serve, what music to play, and what to do with his, um..."

"Body?"

Shorty nodded.

"Am I invited?" Alan asked.

"Of course!" Nathan said, frowning a little, and then he lightened up. "It's this Sunday, seven to nine. Don't worry about anything, Alan, it's all taken care of."

Alan nodded. He looked at Nathan, who was looking sympathetically at him, and thought he'd really rather be alone with his memory. Very, finally and completely alone with his failed and useless love for Monty Vista.

Based on the guest list, the memorial turned out to be more low-key than Alan thought it would. This was probably because there was no open bar or any kind of bar at all. There were lots of flowers and lots of interesting people in

164

mourning. Most of them had been at the party in September. Some of those people were now too sick to come to Monty's memorial.

Toward the end of his life, Monty changed his mind and asked for a closed casket at the memorial. Alan might have done this anyway because the level of deterioration at the end was quite severe. Monty's once handsome face was almost unrecognizable with lesions; he was skeletal and blind and in a coma at the very end.

"I should be used to this," Alan thought. "All my patients die. You'd think I'd be used to it."

There was an eight by ten glossy head shot of Monty in a tuxedo, smoldering in his sexy prime, on top of the casket. This seemed more real to Alan than what was left of his body inside.

The memorial ground on and finally wound down as the last mourners paid their respects and left. The mortuary attendants looked in, and finding Alan lost in thought, went away again. Alan had spent most of the evening waiting for Hackenbush to show up so he could throw her out, but she never did. He felt this was very like her; disrespectful and rude. Well, it was all right; he had something unpleasant to do and here in front of Monty's casket in a deserted funeral home on a Sunday evening was as good a time to break up with Nathan as he could imagine.

He couldn't go on with Nathan. He tried, but Monty's memory—the happy parts, the sad parts, the stupid parts, all of it—stayed in the way. It was like a coil in his chest that just got tighter each day. If he were alone, he'd learn to live with it, but with Nathan... Nathan deserved a better deal anyway. He looked up when Nathan came back from seeing the last mourners off.

"Monty had good friends," Nathan said, sitting next to him. "Somewhat odd... but very nice."

"Very true," Alan sighed. "Look, Nathan..." A door slammed and they both jumped. "Is that a drum?"

They sat up straighter when Hackenbush, carrying her ukulele, Ross, playing a snare drum, Cody and Shorty, carrying nothing, marched solemnly into the room in lock-step. They halted before the casket and turned to face their audience of two.

"You're late, Hackenbush," Alan snarled.

"This is when Monty said to come," Ross said blandly.

Cody waved. "Hi, docs."

"Well, you three are welcome, but Hackenbush can get out," Alan shot back.

"No," she said. "Monty's last wishes were that we come here at nine thirty and sing "Stardust" to whoever's around, if anyone, and then leave. I'm not a Monty Vista fan anymore, but I'd have to be much more of a cunt than I am not to do this one last thing."

"No comment."

Hackenbush shrugged. "Okay, cats; a-one, and a-two–"

"Wait, Mabel." Shorty cut her off. "What about your eulogy?"

"That's got to be the last thing I'd ever want to hear," Alan said, starting to rise and glaring at Hackenbush.

"I'd like to hear what she has to say, Alan," Nathan said quietly.

Alan and Hackenbush stared at each other until the doctor sat back in his seat.

"Look, Alan, I guess I'm supposed to say something philosophical about love or life or the state of the world or something, but I got nothing profound to say. Monty Vista did us both a big favor; he helped me get over a broken heart and hooked you up with the nicest guy he could find, who turns out to be a very nice guy indeed. Monty might have been a bastard and wrong in most ways, but he had more faith in love and art than anyone I've ever known. And even though he wasn't going to live to see it, he wanted you to love and be happy with Nathan. I'm not sorry I was part of Monty's last biggest most important production, because it restored my faith in art, and, seeing what he was willing to do for you, restored a little of my faith in love. Alan, there's enough suffering in the world; you have a chance to make two people very happy—yourself and Nathan—and that's two more than otherwise. Not many get a chance like this, so don't blow it, okay? Ready, cats?

Ross switched to brushes while Hackenbush played a four bar introduction. The guys had learned all the words to

"Stardust" and they sang it simply and straightforwardly to their audience of two doctors.

It was the most beautiful thing Alan Brazil had ever heard in his life. He put his arm around Nathan, who was nearly moved to tears. Monty was right and his messenger was Dr. Hackenbush and her Orchestra, as incredible as that might be. Alan decided he would work it out with Nathan and be happy; mostly for himself and Nathan, but also for Monty and Monty's memory. And even a little for Hackenbush, the bitch, who really was a great singer (too bad about the personality).

"We'll miss you, Monty," Hackenbush said, sidling up to the closed casket. "We'll miss all the guys like you, you rascal, you."

As if for luck, she rapped out the "shave and a haircut" rhythm on the lid. Everybody held their breath until they realized there really wouldn't be the standard "two bits" rejoinder.

Squaring her shoulders, Hackenbush took her place at the head of the reformed cortege, which now included Brazil and Albany, and marched them out of the building.

The mortuary staff were just glad they could finally turn off the lights and go home.

The End

Acknowledgements

As with all the Hackenbush stories, this one would never have seen the light of day without the love, sometimes tough love, and assistance of the wonderful Lynn Loper, Jane Seaton, and Laurel Sutton. If everyone had friends as kind, patient and helpful as these fine ladies, this world would be a utopia.

Special thanks also go out to Robin Austin for the lovely cover, and Kris Anderson and Nancy Lilly for their wise and thorough proofreads of this manuscript.

Stories might be written alone, but they don't take flight as books without the help and support of many people. I'm very lucky that these people are still in my life after everything Hackenbush and I have put them through over the years.

Ladies, I bow down to you. Umbrella drinks for everyone!

Ginger Mayerson
November 2011

www.ingramcontent.com/pod-product-compliance
Lightning Source LLC
Chambersburg PA
CBHW072126170626
46813CB00004B/1715